TRAPPING THE SILVER BEAVER

TRAPPING THE SILVER BEAVER

by *CHARLEY C. NIEHUIS*

ILLUSTRATED BY CHRIS KENYON

DODD, MEAD & COMPANY · NEW YORK

To my boys,

BARRY, DAVID and PAUL

ACKNOWLEDGMENTS

To:

Georgie Daniels who trapped beaver on the Colorado River during the winters of 1944 and 1945, and who actually turned down an offer from contraband fur buyers;

to Black Bart of Maricopa, out of Arodle Peggy by Black Prince of Holly and owned by Eddie Marshall, who could have been a blood brother of Webb's Labrador retriever, Champ;

to Buddy Fox, formerly a game ranger, who was in charge of beaver trapping, and who dreamed of a Division of Fur Conservation for the Arizona Game and Fish Commission;

to Charles C. Bernstein, formerly Juvenile Court Judge of Maricopa County of Arizona for his understanding of boys in trouble; and

to Jim Kjelgaard, himself author of many books for boys, who served as stimulus and conscience in the writing of this book; and most of all

to boys everywhere who at times find it a "rough go" as Webb did, but who, oftener than we realize, turn out right in the end.

CHARLEY NIEHUIS

CONTENTS

ix

ILLUSTRATIONS

TRAPPING THE SILVER BEAVER

ON PROBATION

Webb Dodge pulled himself up and looked across the catwalk and out of the window of the Mohave County jail. He could do this only by stretching his full five-feet-eleven inches, grasping the bars of the tank as high as he could reach, and pulling himself up. The tree on the corner of the Plaza was still green, but near the top the leaves were beginning to turn. The sidewalk underneath the tree was empty of people.

There was still no sign of Brant Murphy and of Champ.

Webb's eyes searched for the sight of the big, golden dog who was, he felt, his only real friend. The bars numbed his fingers and then his arms gave out, and Webb had to let himself down again.

He half-hung, half-stood against the steel bars of the tank in the jail. He closed his eyes and tried to shut out the endless mumbling and monotones of the other prisoners. In spite of the rancid smell of close and unclean bodies and the restless stirring of the confined men around him, Webb felt very much alone.

1

The sight of the tree against the blue Arizona sky, the hope that the game ranger would still come, stirred anew the boy's fierce desire to be free, and brought tantalizing memory-pictures before his closed eyes.

He saw and heard the Slough as he remembered it so well—the water moving quietly in the channel between the endless rows of tules, the booming croak of the bullfrogs, the grating call of the coots as they swam out of the way of his drifting boat.

He shook his head, his unkempt brown hair falling around his lean and now pale face.

"Aw, forget him, Kid," growled a rough voice from a cell adjoining the bullpen. "That game warden won't show up with your dog."

Webb didn't open his eyes or turn his head as he replied, "He'll come. He said he would."

A skeptical snort came from the bunk.

"The law'll let you rot. Brant Murphy's a lawman, even if he's only a game warden."

Webb didn't bother to answer. He'd felt an increasing uncertainty about his Uncle Jake since all this trouble.

It had started on one of those now very rare occasions when he had been with his uncle—almost two months ago it was, he remembered, to the very day. He and Jake had been in a boat, going along the edge of the Slough, when they came upon a cow which had bogged down in the soft, marshy ground and died. On the bank stood a bawling calf, already weak from hunger.

"No use lettin' a good veal go to coyotes," Jake had said, raising his rifle. At the time, Webb had thought his uncle's idea simply practical. He hadn't stopped to remember how serious a crime killing another man's beef was, even today, in this cattle country.

They had just finished quartering the calf when the rancher who owned the cow rode up, steely-eyed and curt.

Two days later the sheriff had arrested Webb and his Uncle Jake. A felony, they had called it during the subsequent trial, and now his uncle was to be sentenced in a few days.

The county attorney had argued that Webb should be tried with Jake, at the same time, but for some reason Judge Schaulkler refused to permit it. Webb had not been able to follow all the legal arguments, but he knew that something Brant Murphy had said or done had influenced the judge's decision.

Webb couldn't figure it out. His old enemy, the game ranger, had accompanied the sheriff when he and his uncle had been arrested. In fact, the game ranger had guided the sheriff to their cabin. Yet, the day Webb and his uncle were booked, the ranger assured Webb that his Labrador retriever, Champ, would be fed and cared for until he could again do it himself. In spite of this kind gesture, Webb had felt nothing but fury at the man who had helped arrest him, and so refused to answer any questions put to him.

"You leave me no choice, Webb," the judge had said regretfully, and so Webb had been jailed with Jake.

A week, two . . . a month went by, and again Webb was called out and in front of the judge. Brant Murphy was there too, and again the ranger began asking a lot of questions which Webb still doggedly refused to answer. None of it was any of their business!

Then Judge Schaulkler had talked to Webb, long and earnestly. The boy's resistance had cracked a little under the firm, kindly reasonableness of the man, and he told how his mother had died when he was just a little kid,

3

and how his father and his Uncle Jake had brought him to Gold Road, where they had gone to work in the Old Glory Hole Mine. He told how his father had been killed in a cave-in which had closed the mine, leaving his uncle without work. Then how his uncle had moved down to the banks of the Colorado River, on the edge of the Slough, taking Webb along.

The boy now stood, leaning against the bars of the tank within the jail, recalling all these things. What good was it to spill everything that way, he asked himself. Maybe Jake was right, maybe they had forgotten him, maybe they never had intended to do anything.

His insides churned, giving him a sick feeling, when he thought about the Slough, the blue sky and the quiet water. He wondered if he would ever be there, ever be off by himself again. He had never wanted anything so much in his life before! Sunk in these thoughts, Webb didn't hear the sheriff's deputy enter the catwalk outside the tank.

"Dodge!" shouted the jailer. "The judge wants to see you downstairs."

Webb raised his head and looked sullenly at the guard, and neither spoke nor moved.

"Get over to the door so I can let you out," ordered the officer impatiently.

Webb stood still, clenching his teeth and trying to think of something bitter to say.

A burly, blond man with an unshaven face pushed out from among the prisoners crowding the cells opening into the bullpen.

"Shake it up, Kid! You heard what the man said."

Webb saw the tank boss spread his feet, poising himself. He had learned soon after being jailed that this self-appointed leader of the prisoners enforced the orders in-

4

side the poorly-managed jail. The tank boss, named Bango, ruled the cell block and selected work crews to do the various chores and so gained favors for himself from the jailer. Webb had learned too—the hard way—that the tank boss was to be obeyed, for his own ears were still swollen from the backhanded cuffing Bango had given him.

The jailer unlocked the door of the tank as Webb came near, and the boy stepped through meekly. He followed the catwalk separating the tank from the wall of the building and waited by the locked door at the end. The jailer behind him called to an officer outside, and the door was unlocked. The two men, one in front and one behind, escorted Webb to the judge's office.

5

Homer Schaulkler, Mohave County's Superior Court Judge, looked up. His brown eyes shone warmly as he extended a hand to Webb.

"Good morning, son!" Then turning to the guards, he said, "Please wait outside and let Mr. Murphy in when he comes."

"Sit down," invited the judge, turning to Webb. "I'd like to tell you something before Mr. Murphy comes, something I don't believe you know. Brant Murphy is your friend—a very good friend!"

Webb pushed his uncut hair back from his pale forehead, but he didn't speak, even though the judge paused to give him a chance.

Judge Schaulkler shook his balding head soberly. "I suppose you believe him to be your enemy, and that's natural. But he isn't, Webb. Believe me, Brant Murphy is one of the best friends you have ever had."

The judge swiveled around in his chair and reached over to the other side of the desk for a folder stuffed with many papers. Webb caught a glimpse of the typing on the front. It was his file. His record!

As Judge Schaulkler turned back he continued speaking in his calm, almost soft voice.

"Brant Murphy came to me the day you were arrested. He's a game ranger, as you well know, but he has studied more law than most officers." The judge nodded soberly, as if agreeing with himself. "Mr. Murphy told me you shouldn't be tried as an adult because he was sure you were under eighteen. But, you will remember you wouldn't tell us your age."

The judge leaned back in his swivel chair as he carefully placed the tips of his well-kept fingers together in front of him.

"In spite of your stubbornness, Webb, and your refusal to answer Mr. Murphy's questions, he still wanted to help you. He appealed to me and that is why I had you brought to my offices for further questioning about a month ago. Remember?" Webb nodded and the judge went on. "The information you gave us then has helped you."

Judge Schaulkler leaned forward and looked sternly at Webb.

"Mr. Murphy was right. You are only seventeen, and a juvenile. That allows me to maintain jurisdiction over you. Otherwise, Webb, you would be tried as an adult, as your uncle has been, and perhaps now you would be waiting for sentencing, as he is, waiting to be sent to prison. In other words, Webb, Mr. Murphy, whom you have regarded as an enemy, is a real friend, your friend! I want you to think that over while we wait for Mr. Murphy to arrive."

Judge Schaulkler turned his attention to a book and began to read, occasionally making notes on a paper in the folder marked "WEBB DODGE."

Five minutes, ten and fifteen passed in silence. The judge remained busy while Webb's confused mind straightened itself out. Finally he could stand the suspense no longer.

"Mr. Schaulkler . . . what are you going to do with me?"

The graying man looked up and smiled reassuringly.

"I think we will know when Mr. Murphy comes." The judge looked at his watch before adding, "He'll be here any minute now."

Webb settled back in the chair. One thing he had learned in the years of hunting and fishing in the Slough was to have patience, and he now disciplined himself to silent waiting.

7

Even before the knock came on the door, Webb's keen ears heard the clicking of a dog's toenails on the floor outside. Then the door opened and a big yellow Labrador walked in. Instantly the somber, dignified office echoed with excited barking and whining as the dog leaped ecstatically around the boy.

Webb slid out of the chair and onto his knees, wrapping his long arms around the wriggling animal. The emotions that he had held securely dammed for two months overwhelmed him. He began to cry silently. Tears filled his eyes and his voice broke as he talked to the Labrador.

"Champ! Champ! Yellow dog. . . ."

Webb dug his tapering fingers in the wire-stiff coat of the dog, pulling the squirming animal close to him.

Judge Homer Schaulkler looked across the pair toward a dapper, smallish man in the uniform of an Arizona game ranger. The officer grinned as he suddenly remembered to remove his Stetson. Automatically he smoothed his already neatly combed black hair touched with gray at the temples.

"Hello, Judge. Looks like we've upset the decorum of your honor's chambers."

Judge Schaulkler smiled and shrugged his shoulders. "Did you and Mrs. Murphy come to a decision?"

The game ranger nodded, raising his hands and clasping them tightly together. "Dora and I are like that about it."

Webb didn't hear or see them. He had his face buried deep in the rough, bristling coat of his dog. Then he felt hands on his shoulders and looked up to see the judge bending over him. The man was smiling and reaching for the Labrador.

"Is this that famous retriever I've heard so much about?"

Webb couldn't say anything for the lump in his throat.

He could only nod. Judge Schaulkler took the Labrador's head in his hands, fondling it.

"He's a fine dog . . . a mighty fine dog. Looks like a champion."

That made Webb feel better and he stood up again. The dog leaped high, still starved for affection from his master.

"Drop," commanded Webb. The dog crouched instantly. Only his golden eyes were alive and eager as he lay, head between his paws and motionless, on the floor.

"Remarkable!" exclaimed the judge. "He's well-trained. You've got absolute control over him!"

Brant Murphy spoke then. "Webb trained him, your honor. I think he has done a good job." The game ranger grinned slyly. "You should see him work for Webb . . . retrieving ducks and geese . . . that's something!"

"I hope to . . . I hope to do just that," replied the judge, looking down at the dog, motionless at Webb's feet. Then the jurist looked up. "I'm sorry, gentlemen, we'll have to push this along. I have a trial set for ten-thirty, so let's get at this matter about Webb here, shall we?"

The judge picked up the sheaf of papers, separating one of them. This he handed to Webb. A quick glance told the boy it was a legal paper, having all the information about him: his father's name, his mother's name, his birth-place, his age, his schooling—Webb knew then that the information he had given the game ranger and the judge had helped him. Too, the paper apparently contained an account of the trouble he had been in, even a report on some of the petty thefts and the many times he had been absent from school during the past year.

"There is your record, Webb," said the judge, looking very solemn. "It isn't very good . . . up to now."

A long, painful silence followed and Webb began to feel

9

nervous and embarrassed. Finally the judge continued.

"This may come as a surprise to you, Webb, but Mr. Murphy has petitioned this court for your probation. I am going to grant it. Now listen carefully. What I have to say now will, I hope, make the difference in whether you become a good citizen or whether you choose a life of crime and imprisonment."

Webb raised steady blue eyes, looking squarely at the judge. Somehow he sensed the importance of this moment without quite knowing why, or how.

"I'm placing you under the guardianship of Mr. Murphy. You are to live with him, or close to him. You are to obey him. He is to be responsible for you.

"You are to report regularly to Mr. Murphy and Mrs. Murphy and to let them know at all times where you are and what you are doing. If you want to go anywhere, or do anything, you must first ask permission of either Mr. or Mrs. Murphy.

"Once a month you are to come to this office, or Mr. Murphy is to come here for you and report on your behavior. As long as it is good, you will have your freedom. If you do anything bad, in violation of the laws of our society, I will have you jailed and you will be committed to Fort Grant, which is Arizona's school for delinquent boys."

As the judge paused, the silence was like electricity in the air.

"Do you understand?"

Webb, mouth tense, nodded his head. His hands were clenched tightly together and he felt confused and uncertain in front of this man who had suddenly turned from warm kindliness to cold severity.

Judge Schaulkler shook his head impatiently.

10

"You will have to learn to speak up, Webb, for your own good. We are your friends here—especially Mr. Murphy— and we will help you *if* you try to help yourself.

"Now, once again—I want you to thoroughly understand this—you are responsible to Mr. Murphy. You must obey him. If you behave yourself until you are twenty-one years of age, I will release you from probation."

The serious expression left the judge's face and he again smiled warmly at the boy and extended his hand. "Now, good luck, Webb!"

"Thank you, sir. Thank you very much," said Webb awkwardly and with difficulty. He felt a reassuring hand on his shoulder as the game ranger stepped closer.

"Okay, Webb? What do you say? Do we make a team?"

Webb nodded his head again, then remembered and said quickly, "Yes, sir!" This time it was easier.

The judge stepped back behind his desk and closed the file marked "WEBB DODGE," saying, "You are free to go now."

Webb could hardly believe what his ears were telling him, but he felt Brant Murphy's guiding hand on his arm, steering him to the door. Almost automatically he snapped his fingers and the Labrador got up and paced behind him as he and the game ranger walked down the hall toward the sunlit door.

2

BANGO, THE BEAVER POACHER

Webb rolled his sleeves a little higher, exposing more of his muscular arms to the fall sun. He noticed his skin, which had bleached to a dirty white during his stay in jail, was a coffee brown again. He felt wonderful. It was just like it used to be, he thought. Everything was turning out just fine since Judge Schaulkler had paroled him.

He realized his feeling about the judge and the game ranger was changing. The judge had given him his liberty, and Brant—as the ranger insisted that Webb call him—had encouraged him to set his traps for muskrats, then had helped him scrape and paint his boat. But probably the best thing that the game ranger had done was to suggest that maybe his young friend would like to live in the little cabin on the narrow neck of land that partly encircled a lagoon on the lower end of the Slough.

The two-room shack had been the Murphys' first home on the Colorado River, some two years ago. It was less than a mile from the ranger's newer and larger house on the mainland. The Murphys seemed to know that Webb would

12

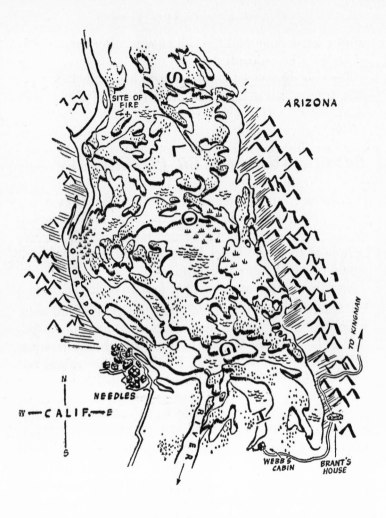

Map of the Silver Beaver region, including the Slough and the Colorado River, bordered by the states of Arizona and California

want a lot of quiet and time alone now, after those weeks of nightmare and confusion.

The only reference the game ranger had made to Webb's past trouble since they had walked out of the judge's chambers six weeks ago was to say, "Stick to the rules, Webb, and you can do anything you want—within reason, of course! Just remember, don't get into any more trouble!"

Webb, as he had done so often lately, realized how good freedom really was. He stretched himself, feeling the heat of the warm fall sun. He sniffed the familiar odors of the Slough. His luck had been good that day, more than two dozen prime muskrats lay under his worktable, in the bottom of the narrow, dead-grass-colored boat. Each pelt would be worth more than a dollar.

The young trapper stood up to look around. This lagoon was completely surrounded by tules, tall water grass higher than his head.

Webb was all alone and deep in the Slough, but this aloneness was good—not like when he had been in jail. Thinking again of the jail, he took a deep breath of the quiet morning air, savoring the somehow clean and not unpleasant mingled smell of green things growing and dead and decaying tules. He sucked it in slowly, filling his lungs.

In front of him, off to the northwest and over the tules spearing the turquoise sky, he could see the shifting towers of smoke above the railroad terminals at Needles, California. He turned around for another look at the thin spires of the mountains to the south and east of him, on the Arizona side of the Colorado River. These were "The Needles" from which the city took its name. He looked at these landmarks so as to establish his own position in the vastness of the Slough. As well as he knew the big marsh, he sometimes became lost in it. But this never

14

frightened Webb. He always knew it would be only a matter of time before he could relocate himself.

Then he smiled down at Champ as he picked up his paddle. The dog was standing spraddle-legged on the deck of the boat.

Webb spoke softly, as he instinctively did when out on the Slough. "This is the life, huh Champ?" The Labrador heard and apparently agreed, wagging his strong tapered tail in acknowledgment, but he didn't turn his head. The yellow dog, ears pricked forward, was intently interested in a coot swimming across the bow as the boat began to move.

Webb reached forward to make a longer stroke. The water swirled under the stern as he forced the craft ahead. He watched the muscles rolling and rippling in his forearms. The boy was proud of his lean strength and he strained to get the boat going fast. He knew that there was only a thin screen of tules separating the lagoon he was in and the hidden channel on the other side. The sharp prow of the narrow craft sliced through the flimsy barrier, and Webb looked up.

With quick, sure thrusts he sent the boat gliding to the far side of the channel where a caliche ridge bank spread fifteen or twenty feet wide and rose whitely three or four feet above the water. Webb scanned the bank for signs of muskrats, but there were none.

Then his nostrils caught an odor in the clean air. He sniffed. There was a sweet, almost sickening smell which was especially strong along the bank. That was beaver! This explained the absence of muskrats, Webb knew. Beaver didn't tolerate muskrats near their colonies because the rats tunneled holes in the carefully built dams and houses.

15

It was a foreign smell—faint, elusive and acrid—that was mingled with the heavy scent of the beaver. Webb paddled silently, back and forth across the channel, holding his head high and testing the air.

He was sure of it now—a man, or men, had passed that way a moment before. Someone who had been smoking a cigar!

Webb heard a warning growl rumble in the throat of his dog. "Drop!" he commanded in a low, firm tone. The Labrador flattened, but peered up the channel, ears lifting.

A thought occurred to Webb. He glanced suspiciously at the nearby channel's bank. The water swirled around his paddle as he turned the boat parallel to it. The clay-like bank was cut here and there with shallow V's running up from the waterline and disappearing in the brush above. Each one of these was worn smooth. Some were filled with tracks, some were moist and slick from recent use.

"Gosh," thought Webb, almost aloud, "a lot of beaver here!"

The air was heavy with the furbearer's sweet, musky scent. The caliche bank, several hundred yards long, was padded smooth along the water's edge by the passing of hundreds of feet.

Webb's keen nose soon led him to a "stink mound." These peculiar piles, built up from hundreds of daubs of mud put there by the beaver, always excited his curiosity. Even now, in his hasty search, Webb marveled anew at the beaver's odd habit of piling up gobs of channel mud on the bank, each new contributor to the pile scenting its own deposit with oil from its musk glands.

The boy's insatiable curiosity had led him to carefully skin out these oil glands from some of the beaver his uncle poached each season. He had found the small pouches just under the skin and on the inside of the hind legs. Surprisingly enough, to Webb, both the boars and the sows had them.

Webb saw that this stink mound was nearly four feet high—a really big one—and again he wondered just why the beaver did this. He grinned as a thought occurred to him—maybe it was a kind of visitor's registry, like a hotel. He made a mental note to tell Brant about the mound and to show it to him the next time they were at this end of the channel together. The ranger would surely be interested—he was always glad to know more about the Slough and its inhabitants; always asking Webb about things he knew. "You've lived here longer than I have," he'd say with a grin.

The boy's thoughts wandered but he continued to paddle quickly from one V-like cut in the bank to another, peering down into the water at each. Then he spotted what he had been looking for!

He reached both hands into the water and grasped the stake he found there and began wiggling it back and forth. Finally he pulled it loose. A wire that led out into deep water was attached to the peg. He pulled on it. The boat rocked as he strained. Then the other end came up, bringing with it a pail filled with cement. Momentarily he fingered the clever locking device that slid up and down the wire. Then he pulled on the trap chain attached to it.

He knew what he would find, even before the drowned beaver bobbed to the surface, its fine, thick fur glossy and dark in the water.

"Poachers." His lips moved silently. "Beaver poachers!"

Hastily he heaved the cement-filled bucket overboard in the spot where he had found it. The dead beaver followed the weight down. Webb carefully replaced the

17

stake at the water's edge. When he paddled away from the bank a few moments later, the beaver set was just the way he had found it.

Unconsciously, Webb began dipping his paddle, holding the boat in position in the channel. He wasn't afraid, still. . . . Muskrat trapping with a license was permitted. He had a license; Brant had seen to that. But trapping beaver was against the law. If it was learned that beaver were being poached in the Slough, it would look bad for him. . . . And after the trouble he had been in. . . .

Then an idea occurred to Webb. He could take the dead beaver to the game ranger. This would clear him of any suspicion.

He discarded the thought almost as soon as it came into his mind. He couldn't take the beaver, that would alert the poachers. They would come soon, running their traps to see if they had caught anything. If the traps were disturbed, they would become cautious.

Should he just tell Brant? Webb's brows drew together, and he shook his head. The idea of "squealing" went against him somehow, but the thought persisted. Mixed with the old feeling that you never gave any help to the law—that getting away with all you could was just common sense—was this new feeling of loyalty to Brant Murphy, the game ranger, and what he stood for.

Webb shook his head again, this time as if to clear it of the conflicting thoughts. He recalled his Uncle Jake saying, "Never trouble trouble 'til trouble troubles you."

Maybe he had better just sit tight and say nothing and things would work out. Webb wasn't really satisfied with this conclusion, but he decided to let it go at that—for now.

He concentrated on the boat and began arranging things, getting ready to travel. He moved all the trapping gear under the worktable. Then he turned and let his outboard motor down and filled the tank with gas. He might need it later and wouldn't want to take time to refuel. Once again, he canted the motor forward on the transom, lifting the propeller out of the water.

As he busied his hands, his mind began figuring ahead. . . . Somewhere upchannel, the poachers were setting or running traps. Reason told him the poachers would be working quietly, so that would mean there wouldn't be any motor noise to warn him. It meant too, that Webb would have to be careful, and quiet!

He was curious, he wanted to see the beaver poachers without being discovered—maybe he would recognize them. Thinking of this made Webb a little uneasy.

He knew the channel he was in entered the upper end of the Slough and flowed for miles, stringing lagoons together and gradually fraying out into smaller waterways and hidden lakes, finally to lose itself in the lower end of the huge marsh.

The lagoon he was in, a part of the channel, pinched out at both ends into narrow waterways that led to other hidden lakes.

Webb swung his ash paddle with quick, sure strokes, ending each one with a twist of his wrists, turning the blade and momentarily using it as a rudder to bring the boat back to its course. As he paddled, he noticed a school of minnows near the surface of the still water; all of them were headed one way. Must be a current here, thought Webb. He neared the upper end of the lagoon. Here it narrowed. The tules grew so close they touched over his head. The knife-like edges of the grass would cut his face so he ducked his head and shielded his eyes with his forearms as he paddled along.

Then, as if coming out of the mouth of a funnel, he glided into the next lagoon. It was too late to be careful. Or to hide!

Over against the caliche ridge, an extension of the one in the lagoon below, there was a boat. A big man was standing in the forward well, hunched over a dead beaver lying on the deck in front of him. In the stern sat a smaller man, looking very much surprised at the sudden, silent appearance of another craft.

Webb's keen eyes took it all in with one swift glance. He saw the look of surprise on the face of the little dark man change to anger.

"Bango, look! A kid!" he yelled to the other.

Even as the larger man jerked erect and turned, Webb knew him. It was the tank boss!

"Well . . ." drawled the big blond man confidently, "Webb Dodge. Heard you got paroled . . . 'fore I finished my time." Here he grinned, his mouth like bent wire in his stubble-smudged face. He dragged the next words out mockingly, "Paroled to a game ranger. Come on over, Kid."

Webb sat motionless. Menace was in every line of the man's tensed body. A growl swelled up in the Labrador's throat.

"Come on, paddle over!" commanded Bango again.

The order took Webb back momentarily to the reeking jail tank where obedience was for the weak, where the strong were obeyed.

The boy sat like a part of his boat, unmoving. The burly man's demeanor changed. His voice grated threateningly as he said, "Listen, Kid! I said, 'Come here.' I want to talk to you."

Even as Webb heard Bango speak, he saw the man move

his hand behind him and waggle a forefinger in a small circle to the other man in the stern. The boy knew what this meant, and he whirled and dropped his own motor. The ten-horse outboard caught on the second pull, even before the little dark man had made his adjustments and pulled the starting rope.

Webb nursed the ten carefully to a full-throated roar. But as his craft began to move, he saw Bango push the prow of the other boat away from the bank and it turned and surged forward. The poachers had an outfit! The roar of his ten-horse was swallowed in the rising thunder of the bigger motor behind him. His own boat, a small light craft, leaped up and out of the water and then leveled off. It began to plane, skittering across the rippling lagoon like a skimming swallow.

He felt a mounting thrill when his boat climbed up on the step, reaching maximum speed. But his exhilaration died quickly. The bigger boat, even with a load of two men, was gaining fast. The poachers had a better outfit.

Webb whipped over in a sharp turn, trying to out-maneuver them, to turn inside. But the bigger craft had too much, too many horses pushing it, and it was superbly balanced. . . . The water of the lagoon was white with froth as the speeding boats slewed around each other. The men were trying to run the boy down!

Webb was desperate. He decided quickly. He had a chance! He knew the Slough. He made a full turn and headed for the tunnel through the tules from which he had just emerged. He was reckoning on losing the heavier boat in the tangle of tules, the lagoons and the shallows that he knew like the two rooms in his cabin.

With an ear-shattering roar, the two boats rocketed through the narrow passageway as if tied together.

In the next lagoon, where he had found the beaver, the boy knew it was hopeless.

The little man skillfully jockeyed the bigger, faster boat around Webb in a burst of speed. The bow wave splashed over the smaller boat, the wake of it lifting Webb's prow. The light, speeding craft flipped, tossing the boy out. For a moment he hung onto the tiller, then fearing the slashing, whirling propeller blades, he let go. Released, his unguided boat roared away.

Webb felt himself being sucked under by the turbulence of the speeding boats. Then he came up to see the poacher's craft turning at the end of the lagoon, coming back at full

speed. They meant to run him down! He gulped air and ducked under and swam down as the boat roared over him, the screw slicing water near his head and filling it with a roaring as he swam underwater for the nearby and screening tules.

Opening his eyes, he could see the shadowy shapes of the tule stumps and he labored his way back among them, his lungs bursting. When he knew he was behind the tules, he turned over on his back and came up, slowly, allowing only his mouth and nose to poke out of the water among the debris. He filled his lungs as he heard the big boat roaring close and submerged again, slowly—like a coot, he

23

thought—and worked his way farther back among the tules.

Finally he had to come up once more. Then he knew he was safe for the moment. The dead tule grass was hanging over the water so thick he couldn't even see out through it—but, he could hear the motor of the poacher's boat as it cruised back and forth, searching for him. Added to his fear for his own safety was his deep concern for his dog. What had happened to Champ since he had been carried off aboard the runaway boat?

It seemed like hours before the men stopped the motor. Their voices came to Webb clearly—the words were as chilling as the water.

"We must have got him on that first pass," he heard the little man say.

"Maybe," agreed Bango flatly, "but I can't take a chance. If that kid'd turn me in, I'd do a long stretch. It'd make my fourth time up!" He paused. "Schaulkler would bury me, so I'm going to search those tules."

Webb heard the squeak and thump of the paddles as the boat was moved to his side of the lagoon. Fear swelled in him and he worked his way down between the tule roots so he could submerge and hold himself down should the men penetrate the protective covering.

Bango threshed around for a long time, probing with the boat and pushing the paddle into the dense growth.

Finally, less than ten feet away, Webb heard the big man speak. "Let's get out of here—I guess we got him!"

"What about the dog? He's still in the boat."

"Leave him," growled Bango. "It'll look more like an accident." There was a pause. It was Bango again. "We must of got him, or he's tangled up in some snags. He sure didn't get away."

24

Webb's heart leaped when he heard the motor start. The throbbing roar went up the channel. Finally it was out of hearing, and in a little while the birds began to chirp again. A bullfrog chugged on the edge of the tules. Webb knew then that it was safe to come out.

3.

ALMOST TOO LATE

Webb swam to the caliche bank and climbed up. Water streamed from his clothing as he stood erect. Chilled through, he clamped his jaws to keep his teeth from chattering. He looked around dazedly, still stunned by the ordeal.

The lagoon was again all peace and quiet. It might all have been a bad dream, thought Webb, except for the broken tules where his boat had crashed through. It was somewhere beyond, he knew that. But where? And how to get to it? And, most important, what had happened to Champ?

Webb knew the Slough too well to dive in and begin a frantic search. He could swim the channel, but beyond that it was mud, soft, sticky mud under a mirror of stagnant water. Often this mud was shoulder deep! There was quicksand too, in places—without a boat the Slough was a man-trap.

He waited a long time, listening and hearing nothing but the swamp noises of fish rising, frogs croaking and the chirp of birds. Finally he decided it was safe. He pulled his lips tight over his teeth and whistled sharply, twice, waited a moment and then repeated the double, ear-splitting blasts.

Webb listened for long anxious minutes before he heard a floundering in the tules. Then Champ heaved into sight, the dog's yellow coat matted with mud. The muscular Labrador, bred for such going, wallowed across another shoal, wormed his way through a screen of tules and swam to where Webb stood.

One look at his exhausted, panting dog told Webb that for him to travel the same route back to his boat would take all the sinewy strength and endurance he could muster.

It was then that he felt the full impact of his desperate situation.

He was miles from the mainland. His runaway boat was deep in the tules. There was no telling how far it had gone before it ran aground or sheared a propeller pin.

Again he looked at Champ for a possible answer. The dog could have come directly from the boat, but on the other hand, he might have jumped from the craft while it was running wild through the tules, and even before Webb whistled he might then have been fighting his way back. There was no telling.

"If you could only talk, fellow!" Webb said, kneeling and scratching Champ's ear absently. If it had not been for his desperate situation, he could have taken pleasure in the time and the place. The lagoon was reflecting the red of the setting sun. Far back in the tules, on the other side of the big oval of water, a largemouth bass rose suddenly, splashing the surface while chasing a school of minnows.

27

Webb clenched a fist. The magic of evening on the Slough was like an evil spell now, and far from pleasant. A line of determination began to define itself along his firm jaw. One thing was certain, he wasn't staying on the comb-like island.

He looked at the sun—almost two hours of daylight left in which to find his boat! Webb knew if darkness caught him bogged down in the silt of a shoal . . . He pushed the thought out of his mind.

He stood up, studied the tules again, tracing as far as he could see the course his boat had taken. As he looked, a bit of willow floated by. This gave him an idea.

He pulled his hunting knife from its scabbard on his hip. In a few minutes he had cut a big armful of willow switches, all about five feet long. Then he took the buckskin strings out of his boots, and working swiftly, he bound and wove the willows into two flat bundles. Then he stripped off his wet clothes and spread them over some nearby arrowweed bushes to dry—no use getting them muddy, and if he got back, he would need dry clothing. Anyway, the going would be easier without their sodden drag.

Then Webb swam across the channel, pushing the two bundles of willows ahead. He called to Champ to follow.

They reached the first clump of tules and fought through. The water beyond was only a few inches deep, but the mud underneath was letting Webb sink to his waist, with no firm footing at that level.

Now he rammed his hands into the two tightly-tied bundles of willows. They held him up and he floundered, swam and inched his way across the shoal.

While he stood, his breath coming hard, he carefully traced the course of his boat from this spot. Again he went on. Swimming, crawling, flopping, he made slow headway, but he took care not to exhaust himself. He rested on the firmer ground when he found it, and at other times he would put his bundles of willows down to stand on them.

Champ lunged along behind him, tongue out, seeming to enjoy the struggle, now that his master was leading the way.

It was hard to follow the course of the boat, but Webb, whose practiced eye could tell a coyote track from a wild cat's in a sand wash, picked it out.

An hour gone, he told himself, as he squinted at the dropping sun. He had long passed out of sight of the caliche bank and he knew now that there would be no returning before dark. He had to find the boat in the next half or three-quarters of an hour, or try to locate firm ground where he could stay until morning. This possibility was one he couldn't avoid thinking about any longer. He wasn't cold now. The shallow, stagnant water had been warmed by the sun. But as the night closed in, it would chill fast. The air temperature would drop almost to freezing.

Webb shivered at the picture in his mind . . . spending the night, naked, wet, on a shoal . . . He didn't want to think of it! The boy wallowed on, trying to move faster now.

He learned he could put one bundle of willows ahead, pull himself over it, then repeat with the other. It was awkward, hard work, though.

Sometimes he found water deep enough for swimming. Then it was easy going, but it was colder, too!

Champ could easily have gone faster, but the dog stayed with Webb. It was almost dark when, all at once, the big Labrador leaped ahead. Webb commanded him to wait, he didn't want a confusion of trails to follow. But the dog was eager.

Webb's legs suddenly felt weak and he strained to see ahead. He felt he must be close to his boat. He put down his bundles and stood on them. There it was, beyond the next screen of tules, where it had driven high on a muddy bar!

Trembling with fatigue and chill, Webb inched the last distance without stopping. He pulled and hauled at the boat, finally floating it, then climbed in and fell exhausted in the bottom. What a feeling to know he was safe at last!

As soon as Webb recovered, he tried the motor. It was wrecked! Then he looked for his paddle. It was under the worktable where he'd pushed it.

It was surprising how short the distance back to the caliche bank really was, and so easy to negotiate in a boat!

Webb tied the craft and searched under his worktable for the matches he kept there. He took his hunting knife and quickly shaved slivers of wood from a dry stick, stacking the splinters loosely in an open space on the bank. One match did the trick and soon a bright, crackling fire leaped up. The surrounding brush caught and reflected the flickering light.

Then Webb dived into the channel and washed the mud out of his hair and from his lean body. He dried and warmed himself in front of the fire. Then he dressed.

As he put on his shirt, a notebook fell from his pocket. It reminded him of something he had to do.

"Wow!" he exclaimed aloud. "I almost forgot."

Quickly he jumped in his boat and examined his motor again. Perhaps he could fix it, but then he saw that the propeller had lost a blade and that the gear housing had been broken in the wild run.

Ordinarily, being without a motor didn't worry Webb greatly. A boat and paddle were all he needed to go anywhere in the Slough. An outboard just helped to get him there faster. Usually, speed didn't mean much to the boy. He had grown up in the out-of-doors where time and distance were things to work with, not fight against. But now, he was in a hurry!

He doused the fire and set out immediately, upchannel, paddling steadily through the narrow waterway and into the wide lagoon where he had surprised the poachers.

His body swung rhythmically with the quick strokes. He would have to go several miles up the waterway before he reached the inlet, then the rest of the trip would be easy!

At the opening of the channel, where part of the Colorado River flowed into the Slough, Webb turned downstream. For a moment he let the boat drift on the breast of the wide river as he caught his breath and rested a while. In front and far off were the reflected lights of the city of Needles, California. The town itself was almost directly opposite the wide expanse of flooded lowland that was the lower end of the Slough.

Not far below, on the Arizona side, was Webb's backwater, the long narrow finger of an old channel that would take him almost to his cabin door.

The river current was sweeping him along at almost seven miles an hour. But, to his impatience, that wasn't fast enough. Gripping the paddle, he dipped the blade and stepped up the cadence of his stroke. He had a long way to go, and he had to get to Brant Murphy's ranch house before daylight the next morning!

In fact, he was already late in making his weekly behavior report to Brant. The days had slid by unmarked—

he had been so absorbed in his trapping. But forgetting wasn't to be any excuse, Judge Schaulkler had warned.

Webb knew he meant it!

Thinking about having to report, Webb decided that one good thing had come out of the whole mess. Brant Murphy had proved to be what Webb hadn't known before—a real friend.

Webb grinned wryly! He'd given his game ranger friend a lot of trouble.

In a sense—at least on his side—it had been a sort of contest between him and Game Ranger Murphy. Webb had hunted ducks and geese in and out of season, from the moment the birds arrived in the Slough each fall, until they left in the spring. He'd had no respect for the boundaries of the federal migratory bird refuges either. The wingshooting provided by ducks and geese had been just a little bit of heaven—and food—in Webb's existence. And since he'd had Champ, the fun of hunting ducks and geese had more than doubled.

Flouting the hunting and fishing regulations had been a game.

Webb remembered the times he had slipped through the Slough just ahead of his "opponent." Sometimes the ranger would catch up with him, other times the officer would give up the game of hide and seek in the marsh and wait for him at the shack where Webb and his Uncle Jake lived. By that time Webb would have hidden his illegal spoil and then he'd stand by and grin while the game ranger searched his boat, to find it clean.

Webb recalled with a sheepish feeling of pride that the officer had really caught him with evidence only twice— once for having too many bass, and another time when he hadn't bothered to buy his hunting and fishing license.

But now Webb was chagrined to remember that both times the doughty game ranger had graciously let him off, releasing the extra bass the boy had in the live box, and buying his hunting and fishing license for him.

Both times Brant had talked to him about the need for conservation and sportsmanship. Somehow the man had kept it from sounding "preachy" and Webb hadn't been nearly as bored and scornful of the lecture as he had pretended.

Reviewing these memories now as he paddled down the river in the stillness of the night, Webb knew a greater liking for the jaunty little man who reminded him so much of a scrappy game cock.

Webb shook his head. Brant Murphy was a peculiar guy! As much trouble as he and Uncle Jake had dished up for the guy, as stubborn as Webb had been when first arrested, Brant Murphy had been in his corner all the time! The game ranger had expressed it that way; he often used terms from the fight ring, where he had once been a lightweight boxer.

With a tight knot in his throat, Webb recalled the first visit the game ranger had paid him in the jail. Brant had brought Champ with him, on a leash, and well cared for! That had really got Webb!

"Don't worry about this pot-licker," Brant had said, leaning forward to pat the Labrador and to adjust the collar while the boy recovered control of his emotions. "We get along fine, and I promise as soon as you get out of this trouble, you'll have him back."

Then, as casually as if they had been sitting side by side in their boats out there in the Slough, with nothing but the blue sky overhead and the swaying green tules around, the game ranger had begun to talk to him.

"Saw a bunch of teal yesterday. First bunch in this fall. Greenwings!" Brant had said. "I was sitting off Dead Cottonwood Point, you know where the big bass hides under that old snag. I was there trying to tease him up when they flew over."

Under the spell of the game ranger's quiet voice, the boy had leaned back, relaxed. The walls of the jail had seemed to dissolve as the officer went on. Webb could see the Point, the snags of the huge cottonwood tree reaching their skeleton fingers up for the fleecy clouds. He saw the teal boring in on set wings, slipping off on first one wing, then the other as they settled, finally dropping their feet just before they hit the water. . . . Suddenly his wonderful daydreams were shattered by a loud, tinny racket! One of the prisoners had clanged his tin cup on the bars of the jail, to call the guard, jerking the boy back to unhappy reality.

He remembered that his voice had cracked a little when he tried to carry on the conversation.

"Have they set the duck season yet?"

Webb could remember every little detail of that miserable day, his yearning to be out . . . free . . . like the ducks themselves.

"Yes," Brant had answered. "I got a bulletin yesterday. Opens the same day as last year, but they added ten more days on the tail end. It closes January 10th. That'll give you a chance at those honkers that come in late every year."

Webb recalled so well what he had said. "No chance for me. I'm stuck."

The game ranger had hesitated, but he hadn't been able to say anything more in reply. Webb's record as a law-abiding teen-age boy had not been good. His card in the

Central Index File had been flagged ever since they caught him hanging around that used car lot. That time he hadn't been doing anything, he was just crazy about boats, and there had been one on the lot, marked "For Sale." No use to tell people that, though, not after he had already been picked up for stealing some hubcaps and other junk which he had sold for nickels and dimes. People always believed the worst.

In a way, Webb blamed his uncle for some of the scrapes he'd got into. But underneath he was honest enough to admit he had known better than to do most of the things he'd done—skip school, for instance.

Still, who'd have felt right in school with the better-dressed kids while the wind was blowing around his legs through torn Levis, or when he could feel the floor through worn-out shoe soles? Any money he got trapping went to Jake as long as they lived together. All in all, it had been a lot easier to hide out in the Slough than to face people who weren't his kind, in the town. Easier—and a lot more fun.

Even so, Webb had found it lonesome business, until that day he found the Labrador pup. It was during duck season—Webb thought back—the one coming up would be the third duck hunting season. He had just turned fifteen. It was the first year Brant Murphy had patrolled the Slough; the game ranger had been assigned to special duty from the central part of the state. Later he had come back on a permanent assignment.

Webb remembered the wintry day he had found the shivering pup marooned on a tule-covered island. It was right at the tail end of the hunting season. . . . Now he looked at the dog, mature, well-trained, sitting quietly on the boat deck in the gloom in front of him.

35

As Webb recalled the finding, a thought occurred to him, a thought that had never registered before—possibly because he'd never really known the game ranger before the last few weeks. Come to think of it now, there had been something funny about the whole deal.

Brant Murphy had brought a hunter over to the shack about a week after Webb had found the pup. He remembered it well, it was the afternoon Champ had learned to retrieve a block; in fact, Webb was working the dog when the game ranger and his companion drove up. The men watched him while he put the pup through his lessons: retrieving, dropping on command, and following at his heels.

The game ranger and the hunter had asked Webb where he'd gotten the pup. The boy had reluctantly given them some information, and some evasive answers. They weren't lies exactly, but . . . Webb felt uncomfortable, even though it had happened about two years before.

Then the officer had led the hunter away and they had talked together, out of Webb's hearing. Finally when they did come back, Brant Murphy had done all the talking.

"We lost a dog, just like that pooch of yours, a little more than a week ago," the game ranger had said, indicating the gangling pup. "He was a purebred Labrador retriever . . . called him Golden Boy . . . as like that pup as peas in a pod."

Webb's heart had almost choked him for a moment, until the game ranger had added, "We're going to keep looking around and see if Golden Boy shows up. If he doesn't, we may want to look that pup over for some identifying marks —since you don't seem to be sure just where he came from." Brant had smiled at Webb then. "I'll keep in touch with you, but you take good care of that pup. Okay?"

They had driven away then, but for a while the game ranger would appear at the shack every few days, to see the dog and ask if Webb had heard of another yellow Labrador showing up anywhere.

Then one day, three months or so later, while Webb was teaching Champ to retrieve out of a boat, the game ranger pulled up in the same lagoon, in his patrol boat.

"Remember that hunter who lost the pup?" he asked after watching the dog work. "He's given up on that lost pup. He bought another Labrador—a yellow one, just like Champ there—a full brother to Golden Boy, the one we couldn't find."

Webb was sure of it—Brant Murphy was quite a guy! Involuntarily, the boy smiled when he thought of his friend and he liked the way he felt—as though he belonged to somebody now, to the Murphys. Unconsciously, he increased the beat with his paddle.

His boat was gliding down the river, silent as the moon shadows cast into the water by the nearby hills. As unerring as a radar-equipped ship coming into a fog-bound harbor, Webb's boat nosed into the lagoon above the narrow spit of land where the Murphys' old cabin was located.

As dark as it was, Webb steered unerringly to the mooring, a partially submerged tamarisk log edging the shoreline. Champ leaped out. Hastily Webb carried the dead muskrats to a worktable set a little distance from the cabin.

Less than ten minutes later he and Champ were trotting along the narrow road that went along the crest of the spit and up to Brant's ranch house.

The sky was just lightening for a new day when Webb came up to the house. It was dark, but he didn't hesitate. He leaped up the three steps to the porch. In the strength-

ening light he saw a note tacked on the door. With the
aid of a match he read:

> "Webb, come in, no matter what
> time you get here.
>
> Brant"

4

THE RANGER CAPTURES WEBB IN A LIE

Webb commanded Champ to lie down on the porch, then stepped inside. He found the gasoline pressure lamp the Murphys used when their electric generating plant wasn't running. He pumped it up and lit it. At first the lamp burned fitfully with a yellow flame, then it began to generate.

He looked around the little kitchen now flooded in white light. Its neatness and cleanliness mirrored the personality of Brant Murphy's wife.

"Who's there?" came from the next room.

"Me . . . Webb."

"Hiya fella!" greeted Brant, coming through the door, hitching at the pajamas twisted around his short but compact and muscular body. Noticing that Webb was breathing hard and perspiring, he said, "You're doing your roadwork awful early . . . or late! What's up?"

Webb felt uncomfortable under the game ranger's direct gaze. He sensed the questions Brant was going to ask.

"No, I'm not in a jam. Honest, Brant! Just late. I . . .

I . . . I had trouble in the Slough," he finished lamely.

Brant gave him a sidewise glance, then said slowly, "Put some water on for coffee. I'll get dressed."

Webb filled the pot with water and set it on a back burner of the butane stove. Then he turned up the flow of oil in the radiating heater. He had washed his hands and was setting the table when Brant walked in, buttoning the form-fitting shirt which accentuated his already wide shoulders, but which stretched at the buttonholes over a slightly bulging middle.

"How about some sourdough cakes, Boy?"

"You bet!" Webb grinned. Brant never forgot his liking for sourdough pancakes and prickly pear cactus syrup! The boy could feel his mouth fill with saliva as he anticipated the breakfast he was going to have.

While Brant was whipping up eggs for the batter, he said, "Make another setup, Webb. Mama's getting dressed." He looked around, partly turning his body because of his stiff neck. "Dora was worried about you last night. Didn't sleep much. When she heard you running down the road this morning, she woke me up."

In a way, Webb liked the concern Mrs. Murphy had for him. Yet it made him feel uncomfortable and was hard for him to understand. He'd been a "loner" most of his life. His uncle had never bothered much about him, one way or the other. And there had never been any women close to Webb since his mother had died; he could barely remember her. Even so, as the boy rearranged the table to make room for Dora Murphy, he felt a strange warm glow inside. He switched two of the chairs around, giving her the more comfortable one.

Then she came in, a neat, young-faced, white-haired woman. She laughed as she put her arm around Webb, even though he was head and shoulders above her. She gave him a quick hug.

"We expected you last night, Webb. Did something go wrong?"

Webb saw the game ranger turn, waiting for him to speak.

"Lost a blade on my prop and cracked a gearcase housing on my motor," Webb explained, instinctively falling into the old habit of hiding the real reason from the law enforcement officer. "I had to paddle all the way back."

"First time I ever heard of you running onto a shoal." Brant laughed. "You've always bragged how you could run the Slough in the dark and never shear a pin!"

Webb squirmed in his chair. He got up to mask his embarrassment. He wondered why he had covered. Now that deception was started, he had to keep it up! He tried to think of something to say, to change the subject.

"Say, Brant, I'd like to show you a real big stink mound I found yesterday."

"Stink mound!" exclaimed Dora. "What in the world is that? Sounds awful!"

The game ranger laughed as he stacked four pancakes and set them in front of Webb. "There's a starter, Son. But you'd better tell Mama what a beaver's stink mound is before you eat. She won't leave you alone until you do!"

As Webb buttered his flapjacks and poured the rich red syrup made from the fruit of the prickly pear cactus over the golden cakes, he told about the mound he'd found. When he finished he added, "There's a lot of beaver in the Slough, Brant. Why can't a fellow trap them? Beaver pelts are 'way up in price."

The game ranger did not reply right away. He poured

41

a cup of coffee for his wife and Webb, then filled his own.

"Funny thing, I've been wondering about those beaver myself." Brant spooned some sugar in his coffee and stirred it noisily. "Beaver have been protected ever since the Arizona Game and Fish Commission was created—that's the state agency set up to protect the wildlife, Webb. The members of the Commission, and the Director too, say unlimited beaver trapping is not a good idea. They argue that, because of the high prices beaver pelts are bringing, there would be too many trappers, and too many beaver would be caught. But right now the Commission has its own trappers catching beaver up in the White Mountains, on the head of the Little Colorado River, where there is an overpopulation. Some of the small ranchers and farmers up there are complaining about beaver damming up the irrigation ditches." Brant turned from the pancake griddle, waving his spatula. "But you know, I don't believe the Director, nor the Commission, know they've got a flat-tail over here on the River!"

"Haven't they made a beaver survey on the Colorado?" asked Dora.

"No, they haven't," replied the ranger as he put three more hotcakes on Webb's plate, grinning when the boy looked up. "Line your ribs with those saddle blankets, Son. I want to get you into the light-heavy class by spring." Turning to his wife, he said, "They've never had a game ranger based over here before."

Suddenly the ranger leaned forward. "Say, I've got an idea." Waving his cup, spilling a little coffee in his enthusiasm, the officer went on, "Webb, could you, would you spring your muskrat traps and go with me for a few days and make a beaver survey of the Slough and the River above—maybe up as far as Bull's Head or Cottonwood Island? I'd like to get an idea of how many beaver there are. You could guide me. I'd pay you day wages."

Webb's heart beat double time. Guiding! That was the one thing he had always hoped to be able to do, to take hunters out during the duck and goose hunting season and to hire out as a guide for fishermen who didn't know the Slough! What was the game ranger up to? Did he suspect something? Was he setting a trap? Webb wished he hadn't deceived Brant as to the real reason why he had been late. Now he wished he had been straightforward about the whole thing. He had to say the first thing that came into his mind.

"But you know the Slough, Mr. Murphy. You know it as well as I do. You don't need a guide."

The ranger lit his pipe, drew on it a couple of times as he pondered the things Webb had said. Then a slow smile spread across his face, parting his lips and showing the neat band of gold around two front teeth.

"First off, I want you to chuck that 'Mister' . . . call me Brant . . . all the time!" He pointed his pipestem at Webb, emphasizing what he was saying. "You can be a real help to me, and I'll pay you for it."

Webb shook his head stubbornly, still not understanding the ranger's motive. He countered with, "You know the Slough."

Brant became serious, hitched his chair toward Webb. "Sure, I know it—like a part-time sportsman might. But . . . and I'm not bringing this up to make you feel bad, Webb . . . but I chased you around in the Slough for the best part of two years, trying to catch you in a game law violation." He jabbed his pipestem at the boy, "But you always gave me the slip, didn't you?"

Webb nodded. His face was a mask at the reference to those days when he'd been at war with Brant Murphy. But, still, along with his embarrassment, he felt a curiosity. Still he said nothing.

"Okay," continued Brant. "No argument on that—you know the swamp better than I do. Now if I had spent all my time here on the Slough, I'd probably know its wildlife and where to look for it, but I've had a lot of country to patrol—the Hualpai Mountains—the Arizona Strip—all the country south of Lake Mead—the upper end of Big Chino and Lonesome Valleys—I've just had too much territory and too little time." The game ranger hitched his chair closer to Webb. "I can hire you as a guide and boatman and as a technical expert on beaver, and the game department would be getting its money's worth!"

Dora Murphy leaned across the table and put a hand on Webb's arm. "That's right, Webb. You can help Brant."

As soon as Mrs. Murphy spoke, Webb knew Brant's offer was genuine, and inside he felt a little ashamed that he hadn't trusted the man who had already proved to be his friend.

"Okay, I'll go," he said, "but," he shook his head unbelievingly, "to think of getting paid for that!"

"Good!" said the game ranger, rising. "Now we've got things to do!" He turned to his wife, "Dora, will you lay out enough chuck for a four-day campout, please? Don't forget! Put in a jar of sourdough starter. My guide will want his hotcakes!"

Webb listened, smiling to cover his mixed feelings. He was happy, in a way, happier than he could ever remember being, yet he felt a shame for having deceived his friend about his delay in the Slough. He wondered now why he had and became so lost in thought he didn't realize Brant was speaking to him until the ranger touched him on the arm.

"What's the matter, Kid? You look like you've been stealing sheep."

Webb flushed, laughed nervously. "I'll still . . . I was still thinking . . . getting paid for guiding a game ranger!" he said quickly.

Brant smiled, nodding his head slowly, knowingly. "That's all right. Laugh about it if you want to . . . but not now! Take my truck back to your cabin. Get things buttoned up and have some sleep. I'll load here and come through the Slough by boat. I'll be at your place at daylight, tomorrow. Okay?"

"Yes, sir!" exclaimed Webb, leaping up. Then he laughed. "I guess you do need a guide, Brant. You can't make it around through the Slough by boat and over to the cabin in much less than two hours. I'll see you between eight and nine o'clock." Then he turned and said, "Goodbye, Mrs. Murphy."

He and the game ranger went out into the yard, and he took the truck.

Fifteen minutes later he was back at his cabin. First he skinned the muskrats and stretched the pelts. Then he buried the carcasses deep in the ground, far from his cabin. That finished, he fed Champ.

Suddenly he felt overcome with fatigue. He had been without sleep for over thirty hours. Tired as he was, though, he forced himself to sweep out his cabin and to clean the ground around it. The cabin was his, in a sense. It was home, so keeping it clean was somehow a good feeling. He put everything in order, then he pulled off his clothes and fell on his bunk bed.

When Webb woke up he was aware of a faint light permeating his cabin. He thought he'd slept through the afternoon and that it was dusk. He reached up alongside his pillow for his flashlight to look at the clock. When he saw the time, he leaped out of bed. He'd slept the clock around and then some! It wasn't getting dark, it was the morning light creeping into the cabin!

Webb dressed hurriedly, stepping outside as he pulled and squirmed into his Levis and buttoned them. He listened for Brant's motor. The Slough was quiet.

Webb felt his dog walk close and lift his muzzle, pushing the cold wet nose into his hand for a caress. As the boy rubbed the retriever's ribs, Champ stretched, first his front quarters and then his hind legs, moaning a little in pleasure. Webb knelt beside the yellow dog and put an arm around him, then he looked out across the lagoon in front of his cabin.

The water was glass-still, mirroring the purple of the early morning sky. The surface was flecked with brown, little rafts of floating bloom from the cattails on the far side. A coot swam out from the shielding grass, croaked a couple of times and then disappeared. Out through the end of the lagoon, through the opening leading onto the river, Webb could see that the sun was just touching the mountains on the California side of the Colorado, bathing them in a red-gold light.

Webb was as quiet as his surroundings. The early morning and just before dusk were the times of day that he liked best. His only movement was to run his long fingers over the rope-like muscles covering the broad shoulders of his dog.

He was reluctant to move, but he knew he had to cook himself some breakfast. He got up and built a quick fire in the wood stove. When he had finished and was tidying up the corner of the cabin that served as his kitchen, he heard Champ growl a warning. Webb stepped to the door and listened. Far away, in the distance, he could hear the soft, steady puttering of an outboard motor. It was Brant, working his way through the Slough!

It was some time before the game ranger turned into the lagoon. Webb rolled his bed and knotted a rope around it. He carried it down to the tamarisk log imbedded at the shoreline as Brant swung into sight. The boy pushed his own boat out of the way, and the ranger drove his sleek, new craft alongside.

"Hiya, fellow!" Brant gave his usual cheerful greeting. "Got your bed rolled and ready to go, huh? Say, you were right! It would put kinks in a snake, that route by boat from my place over to here."

Webb grunted as he heaved his bedroll up and placed it crosswise, just back of the front seat.

The game ranger laughed at the boy's red face. "Man, you must have that thing loaded with soogans. That's a Montana bedroll!" Then he asked, "Where's your fishing tackle?"

"I thought we were working on this trip?"

"Sure we are, but we've got to eat, and part of that work will be to catch a bass for our supper! Scram now, and get it."

Webb dashed into his cabin and gathered up his tackle box and casting rod. Then he and Champ got in the front well of the boat. The ranger stayed in the stern, where he ran the motor and guided the craft.

It was some three hours later, three hours of threading the boat through narrow waterways and lanes, over shoals and around bars—and they were still crossing the lower end of the Slough. They were deep in the swamp and had stopped momentarily in a narrow lagoon, a patch of open water completely surrounded by tules.

"It beats me, Kid, how you find your way around."

Webb hesitated, then grinned, looking straight at Brant. "You learn these back routes, quick, when you're trying to stay out of the way of a game ranger."

Brant nodded soberly. "Yes, I suppose you do, but that's over with now. Isn't it?"

It was a moment before Webb could reply. He said, "Yes, sir . . . it sure is." Brant hadn't reacted in his usual way.

"Where's that stink mound you were telling me about?" asked the game ranger.

Webb stood up in the boat. Through the tules he could see another waterway ahead.

"We can push the boat over this shoal and get into deep water if you tip the motor up. The mound's about a fifteen-minute run up that channel."

They heaved and strained together. Finally they rocked the loaded boat over the mud bar and Brant dropped the motor and started it. The watery, steady chuckle of the motor had a pleasing liquid sound to Webb. He leaned back against the bedroll.

White clouds, reminding him of loose bolls of cotton, were floating in the blue, blue sky. The sun was warm on his back. It had been a day to enjoy, but in the last few minutes Webb had detected a change in Brant's attitude. He didn't dare, didn't want to look around.

They navigated a bend and entered the lower end of a bigger, wider lagoon. Webb knew exactly where he was. The stink mound was on the caliche bank that came into sight. Then he thought of the beaver poacher's set. It was just beyond the mound. Would the drowned beaver still be there? He wished again that he had told Brant the real reason why he had been late. Now he wanted to tell the ranger about the poachers, and to show him the beaver, but . . .

"Smell the beaver?" he asked Brant. Then, without waiting for a reply, he pointed to the caliche mud bank. "Over there, there's the mound. Pull in a little closer and I'll show you some beaver sign."

Webb pointed out the innumerable slides. As they cruised slowly along, he indicated stumps of willows and small cottonwoods the beaver had left after cutting down the succulent young growth. Then they came to the stink mound, rising above the brush.

The game ranger ran the boat into the bank, leaving the motor in gear and idling, driving the craft forward with just enough force to hold it steady into the bank while he stood up in the stern and took a picture of the curious pile of mud.

"It's only a record shot, for my report on this survey," Brant explained.

They moved on a ways. Then suddenly Brant shut off the motor and stood up.

"Say! Somebody had a fire up on the bank there—not long ago!"

"I did," Webb replied without thinking. "Night before last. I dried my clothes there."

"You did?" asked the ranger smoothly. "You didn't say anything about being dumped."

Webb felt his neck get hot. He felt the red creep up under his collar. It began to burn alongside his face.

"Okay, Webb. How about coming clean? Just what did happen here day before yesterday?"

5.

A CODE OF UNDERSTANDING

A sudden terror gripped Webb. He felt trapped inside a dreadful silence where the birds had stopped singing. The water that had been rippling and chuckling under the boat a moment before seemed to turn to oil that flowed silently.

He swallowed hard, but the knot stayed in his throat. All the laughing glibness he used to have when the ranger questioned him was gone. He struggled for words. None came. All he could do was to sit there and silently open and shut his mouth.

A painful moment passed. Then Brant spoke again. There was a hardness, a finality to his tone that Webb had never heard before.

"I want you to level with me, Webb. Something happened to you day before yesterday that you haven't told me about. I looked your boat over this morning while you were getting your fishing tackle. You were running fast when you had your accident—something *you* don't do in the Slough. The keel is damaged. The bottom is scarred.

You had to be going, going fast, to crack a gearcase housing. You were in water, and in mud. You've still got some inside your ears."

Webb's hands flew to his ears. A bit of crusted mud was just under the fold of each one!

"Now Webb, I want it clean, or I'm getting out of your corner."

The boy labored with his words, trying to make an explanation. They dragged out haltingly, at first, then, as he talked, the story came easier. When he had finished, Brant leaned forward and took out his pipe. He carefully tamped some tobacco into it. Slowly, deliberately, he selected a match from a handful he dug out of his pocket and lit the straight-stemmed briar.

Then he looked directly at Webb. "You didn't have a thing to hide from me. You don't have a single reason for protecting Bango—in fact, you had every reason in the world to tell me all about it even before I asked—for your own protection." Brant took a puff on the pipe, thought a moment, then spoke calmly and without feeling. "Frankly, it sounds like a wild yarn."

He stopped, studying Webb through the blue smoke rising from the pipe.

The boy fought for control of his racing, jumbled thoughts. Only one stood out. He had to convince his friend that he wasn't covering or lying now.

"I'll show you the beaver—the trapped beaver," he almost stammered in his eagerness. "It's over there. That's where . . ." The terrifying thought shot through his mind: what if it wasn't there!

"Okay," said Brant, turning to pull the starting cord. "Where do we go?"

Webb pointed up the channel. The ranger guided the

51

slowly moving boat to the foot of the slide Webb indicated. The boy crawled out on the deck and lay flat while he reached down into the water, feeling for the stake. His fingers groped along the silt bottom. There was nothing!

The trap was gone! The set had been pulled.

Webb fought for composure as he said, "They must have taken it yesterday."

There was no response from the ranger.

"Maybe I can find another set," suggested Webb hopefully.

But he couldn't find another trap. He searched all along the caliche bank, even up in the next lagoon, where he had surprised the poachers. Bango and his companion had pulled them all!

Finally Brant shut off the motor.

"Webb, I want to tell you something before we go any farther," the ranger said, pausing to light his pipe again as he thought of what he was going to say. "That's a pretty fancy story, and frankly, I don't know whether to believe you or not. Yesterday, I would have—I had faith in you. You've got to have faith in a person to believe him." Brant stopped a moment. Webb's world closed in on him, as it had when he was in jail. "You lied . . . well, not exactly lied, but you didn't come clean about this . . . and gosh knows why. I don't. But—I still have faith in you."

Brant gave something between a nod and a shake of his head, as though he were undecided. Then he straightened.

"I don't know what you've been up to, but as I said, I'm sticking with you. If you're on the level, in time, the whole thing will come out."

The ranger rapped his pipe on the gunnel of the boat, knocking the ash out of it.

"But, one more thing. Just another fib to me and I'm

turning you back to Judge Schaulkler. If you want me in your corner, you're going to have to come clean with me. From now on! Got it?"

Webb nodded, his mind whirling with scenes of what had happened to him. All of them centered around one, the game ranger as he was now, eyes slightly narrowed, lips pulled tight and his determined jaw shoved forward belligerently.

Then Brant's severity dissolved in a smile. "Okay, let's hunt beaver!" He turned and pulled the starting cord. The motor roared up unevenly then smoothed out as it was throttled down.

The boat began to glide forward on the smooth water. The ranger shoved his hat back and started to whistle.

The next few hours were the worst Webb had ever lived, even more so than the first ones he had spent in jail. He knew that this time his trouble was of his own making. He couldn't blame his uncle, or anyone but himself. Silently he made a vow, that he would regain the complete confidence of the man behind him.

Webb strained for the easy feeling of comradeship that had existed between them. He pointed out beaver sign: the slides, the cuttings, the feed pads. He searched every bank for tracks, for tunnels opening underwater and leading back and up into the bank where the beaver made their dens.

It was getting toward late afternoon and they were running at less than half-speed along a channel in the upper end of the Slough. Webb saw a telltale V in the water, the flat head of a swimming beaver. He pointed it out to Brant. The ranger swung the boat over, to move alongside. When they neared the beaver, it seemed to curve half out of the water, then it disappeared in a dive. As it went under, the broad tail flipped up and slapped down on the surface of the water with a pistol-like report.

Almost instantly from back in the tules two other beaver passed on the warning of danger. Then a fourth spatted the water.

"Boy!" exclaimed Brant, voicing surprise. "There are lots of them."

"A lot more than you'd guess," said Webb, feeling almost himself again. He found more beaver sign for the game ranger than he himself had realized there was.

Now, up ahead, he saw two small islands that had been overgrown with willows. The growth had been cut off by beaver until there was only a stubble of sprouts a few inches high. "Look, Brant, there are so many beaver here they've eaten themselves out of willows."

Brant shut off the motor, letting the boat drift.

"That's what I've been thinking, Webb. I'd never have believed there were so many beaver as you've shown me today."

The ranger took his pipe from between his teeth, "I've never seen the Slough before, been too busy checking hunting and fishing licenses and trying to catch up with the game law violators."

The boy flushed. Brant looked up, then down at his pipe, hastening to say, "Wait, Webb. I didn't mean it that way!"

The ranger continued. "The Commission passed a new order at their last regular meeting. They made conservation officers out of us rangers. We're supposed to make investigations and suggestions for better wildlife management in our districts. This trip is convincing me we had better harvest them."

"Harvest beaver?" asked Webb.

"Yes. That's just another way of saying, trapping beaver.

But it seems to mean more. Any kind of animal can become too plentiful in a certain area, like the beaver here. If they aren't thinned out or cut down in numbers by trapping, or predators, then Nature will step in and cut them down by disease or starvation."

It was a new line of thinking for Webb. He kept silence, pondering over what Brant had just said. At last he was seeing his erstwhile enemy—the game department, the U. S. Fish and Wildlife Service—in a new light. And Brant and the other rangers for the state and federal government were a lot more than the country cops, snoopers and spoilsports he used to consider them. They were working for something—good—hard to do.

"You mean that we . . . that I might be able to trap beaver?"

Brant leaned back against the motor.

"I don't know about that. Maybe the Commissioners won't see it that way. From what I've seen today though, I'd say it would be smart to crop the beaver . . . trap them," Brant added, smiling. "But just how they'll take them . . ."

The rest of what Brant was saying was lost in a ponderous splash near a clump of tules. A bass had erupted from the surface, sliding half his length up a tule stump to snap at a flitting bird which had ventured too close to the water.

Both Brant and Webb sat up, startled!

"That reminds me," said the ranger, reaching for his tackle box. "We've got to catch a bass for supper and it might as well be him!"

Although Webb had fished for largemouth bass many times, he would rather watch the ranger fish than do it himself. Brant was a past master of the short casting rod.

The ranger took a glass blade out of its case and fitted it into a handle, screwing down the chuck. The fittings and the line guides, made of polished chromium, caught the light of the setting sun. Brant used a narrow-spooled, light metal reel, Webb noticed, instead of the cumbersome kind he had. As he watched, Brant threaded the line through the guides and selected a plug from the tackle box.

"Think he'll like this one?" the ranger asked with a grin.

Webb nodded, he was almost comfortable in the officer's presence again.

To Brant, fishing was a sort of rite. He elevated the rod tip, reeling in the line until the lure was snug against the tip guide, turning his wrist so that the reel was spinning on its axis when he cast. Then he sighted over the lure to the base of the stump. He flicked his wrist. The rod whipped up. The lure flashed in a tight circle over the fisherman's head and shot with rifle-like accuracy to the place where the bass had risen.

Brant let the lure rest where it fell. The splash rings spread out and disappeared, and still the ranger waited, slowly reeling in the slack line. Then he flicked the rod. The cupped face of the lure threw up a bubble of water which burst noisily.

At that . . . the bass came up!

The fish slashed out in a smother of foam, carrying the lure up in his mouth. He stood on his tail, shaking it, like a terrier with a stick, the treble hooks rattling on his horny gill covers.

"Yowiieeee!" yelled Brant as the largemouth fell with a splash and made a run.

Webb glowed inwardly. This was like it used to be!

The bass looped out into deeper water, the tight line

zizzling through the floating cattail bloom like a hot knife. The fish chugged against the resilient rod like an angry bull on the end of a lariat. The reel handle spun in Brant's hand. Then the bass ended his run.

"Wow!" whooped the ranger. "He's full of fight!" Brant pumped the rod, lifting the sulking bass. The fish came up in another leap, but the flexible rod took up the slack, holding the lure tight against the hooks set in its lips. Soon the bass tired and Brant eased it alongside the boat.

Webb watched closely. He had seen Brant pick up a hooked bass before, but he wanted to see it again, to see just how the ranger did this.

Brant pulled the tired fish through the water with his rod. Then he reached down, gently eased his thumb into its gaping mouth and at the same time slipped a finger under the flared gill cover. Then he gripped hard, picking up the bass in the same motion. It hung limp in his hand.

"Bass fillets for supper, Webb," chortled Brant. "Now let's find a camping spot. I'm hungry!"

Webb knew of an island nearby that would be just right. It rose some dozen feet above the Slough. It was high enough so that the wind could sweep it clear of mosquitoes. Brant beached the boat in a little cove and Webb tied it fast. Champ leaped ashore, frolicking and hurrying to explore the island.

The man and boy set to work making camp, each to his own tasks, carrying the bedrolls to high ground, clearing the area of sticks and stones and gathering wood for the evening fire.

Webb took out his sheath knife to clean the fish, gutting and gilling it with swift, deft cuts. Then, without scaling the bass, he sliced off the fillets. This done, he turned each slab of meat, skin side down, onto a smooth, clean piece of driftwood. By sliding the thin, sharp blade of his knife along the underside, he cut the skin away from the silvery white flesh, leaving the slabs of meat clean and ready for the frying pan.

By the time he had finished, Brant had assembled the gasoline stove, had it pumped up and lit. Webb settled himself, leaning back against his unrolled bed, and watched his friend prepare supper. As he observed the scene in front of him—Brant hunkered down over the hissing gasoline stove, frying fish—he thought of the day's events, and again resolved to regain the confidence of the ranger . . .

The next thing Webb knew, Brant was shaking him awake.

"Golly, you did that quick. Thanks!" the boy muttered, struggling to sit erect so as to take the plate of food Brant offered him.

After they had eaten, Webb washed the dishes while Brant started the campfire. The ranger placed his unrolled bed close to the mounting flames and sat down with his back to the fire.

"I'm going to build myself one smoke, talk to you a little bit and then I'm going to roll it out," he said.

The boy's mind snapped to attention. He felt the game ranger was going to refer to the day's events, but Brant's talk took another track.

"Webb," he said after he had his pipe going, "I want to point something out to you—something I don't believe you realize yet. . . . As you grow older, you're going to hear a lot about the need for truth. The world and the people on it have got to have truth, otherwise we'll destroy ourselves."

Brant studied the glowing fire at his feet for a moment, then continued.

"Let's take this beaver survey we're making as an example. You and I could spend our time fishing and fooling around—doing very little actual work. Couldn't we?"

Webb had to agree to that.

"We could dream up a false report of some kind, maybe recommend unrestricted trapping, or no trapping at all. No one would be the wiser, until it was too late! If somebody didn't catch up with our lie, the beaver would suffer. Either they'd be trapped out because of our lie, or a lot of valuable fur would be wasted because the beaver would die from some epidemic or from lack of food. What I want to get at, to point out to you—and I don't know whether I've made it clear—is that the most worthwhile thing a person can do is to tell the truth. If people would, could, be completely honest, it would clear up lots of the troubles in the world. Maybe the finest thing we can do for each other is to be honest, square."

The ranger crossed his legs under him, and rocked forward to knock his pipe out. Then he got up and undid the rope around his bed and rolled it out flat.

Webb saw him smile quietly, his warm eyes catching the flickering light of the campfire.

"That's the end of the sermon. Good night, Kid. I'll see you in the morning."

Webb rolled out his own bed and separated his blankets. Without thinking what he was doing, he went through the motions of pulling off his Levis, rolling them up and tucking them under the head of his bed where they would serve as a pillow. His mind was grinding up what the game ranger had said. He was doing his best to understand it. Surprisingly it all made sense. If he couldn't be honest with his own best friend. . . . If Brant couldn't believe him, who else would?

59

6.

STRANGE VISITORS TO THE CABIN

Webb woke when Champ uncurled. The big dog was standing up on the foot end of his bed, stretching. It was early morning. The boy lay listening in the quiet and then caught the soft, rhythmic whistle of beating wings. He looked up to see a curving, wavering line of pintail ducks winging low over the island.

He stretched luxuriously, his shoulders pushing out from under the blankets into the crisp air. Then he laced his fingers behind his head to raise it a little, so he could follow the sprigs in their flight across the Slough.

"Pretty sight," said Brant unexpectedly from his bed on the other side of the dead fire. "Low-flying ducks against a morning sky."

"I'll say!" agreed Webb, sitting up in his bed and feeling for his rolled Levis under the bottom blanket. He bounced up quickly in the cold morning air and pushed his bare feet through the twisted Levis. "Stay in bed. I'll make some hot coffee."

"Ha!" snorted the ranger. "Any time I let a fuzz-faced kid nurse me in bed!"

The boy laughed to see the officer shivering in the light but cold wind, fighting to get his feet through his pants legs. Webb felt wonderful. He had awakened with a new purpose in life. The day promised to be bright and sunny. Brant semed to be his jocular self. . . . And, at the first opportunity—the first time he could do it without the game ranger seeing him—the boy curiously rubbed the back of his hand against his cheek; his whiskers had a stiffness to them!

An hour later, Webb pushed the boat away from the island and they were soon putt-putting slowly through the lagoons and channels. They crisscrossed the upper end of the Slough. Here the Colorado wasn't as wide as it was below, at the lower end of the Slough.

Webb took special note of the newly-formed bars. Many were bare of vegetation. He looked them over carefully, noticing their shapes and their positions in the river. In his eagerness to see better, he half raised himself in the boat. Then he heard Brant idle the motor.

"Some good goose hunting bars here!"

"Perfect," said Webb, his eyes lighting up. "You could make a blind in that pile of dead timber—over there in the middle, on that high ground. That would be the spot! You could string your decoys along the upper end, up there."

"Keep it in mind, Webb," said Brant. "There should be some honkers down in another thirty days—just as soon as it storms up north around Jenny Lake and Bear Lake, in Utah. Then let's take Judge Schaulkler goose hunting. Okay?"

Webb nodded agreement and grinned at the idea of a parolee taking his judge hunting as he idly scratched the ears of the Labrador sitting next to him. The thought of hunting ducks and geese again was very pleasant to the boy.

Brant shoved the throttle over and the boat surged ahead. They spent the rest of the day exploring both banks of the river and all the main backwaters of the upper end of the Slough. They made countless observations of beaver sign.

This was a new experience for Webb. Toward the end of the day he felt as if he had answered hundreds of questions about beaver. . . . Things that had never seemed important before came to his mind under the persistent questioning of the ranger, things about beaver that he had seen himself and that he had heard his uncle describe. These must have all been interesting to the game ranger because he made many notations in his notebook as Webb talked.

They spent another night in camp—this time on the bank of the river, above the head of the Slough.

It was well past noon on the last day of the survey when Webb looked at his watch. He had guided the ranger to a narrow stretch of the Colorado, where it formed the boundary between Arizona and Nevada. The boy waved his hands, drawing Brant's attention to the high, multi-colored sandstone cliffs on each side.

"Painted Canyon. The river widens above, and then we'll come to Cottonwood Island. We can camp there tonight, and make it back home tomorrow."

"That's jake with me," replied Brant. "I've seen about enough."

Webb groaned as he stood up in the boat for a moment, stretching his long legs, "Three days in a boat sure puts a crick in my knees."

"Let's take a straight run up to Cottonwood Island and make camp," suggested Brant, shoving the throttle over.

"Okay!" Webb laughed, leaning back and feeling the wind in his face. The roaring motor pushed the sleek boat up on the step. But, even in his keen enjoyment of speed, the boy didn't forget to keep a sharp lookout ahead for snags and gilhoolies, those shifting sandbars in the river.

In another hour the pair were carrying their gear ashore and making camp under some huge cottonwoods. Webb and Champ explored the island—a long, flat, egg-shaped rise of land that lay in the middle of the Colorado River. The boy took this opportunity to put the Labrador through several retrieves, sending the big dog out into the swift-flowing water after thrown blocks of wood.

It was after supper—after Webb had finished the dishes and while the ranger smoked his pipe—that Brant took out his notebook again. The boy watched him do some more writing in it.

"You've almost got a book there."

Brant laughed. "Sure have. I've learned plenty on this trip. Webb, you know you ought to do something with that knowledge you have about beaver."

"I don't see how . . . except to trap beaver," said Webb, feeding another stick of wood into the campfire.

"I'm not so sure," replied Brant slowly.

The boy could see that the ranger was thinking.

Then, after a while, Brant spoke again. "You seem interested in what I've been putting in my notebook. Would you like to hear my ideas?"

"Sure would!" exclaimed Webb, instantly curious.

"I'm going to recommend to the Commission that we have limited trapping of beaver in the Slough, and that

63

we clean trap the river from Davis Dam site at Bull's Head to Boulder Dam."

"An open season?" asked Webb eagerly.

"Not exactly, but a supervised trapping project." Brant cocked his head. "At least that's the way I see it."

Webb couldn't hide his disappointment. It sounded like the same old run-around. "You mean I don't get to do any . . . just some state trappers will get in on it?"

Brant filled his pipe, thinking a moment.

"Just a minute, Webb. Let me explain my idea. The beaver were practically exterminated when Arizona became a state—and that hasn't been too long ago—1912, if you don't remember your history. Even at that, it wasn't until the 1930's that the game department began doing anything for beaver." Brant stopped a moment and tamped the tobacco down into his pipe. "The hunters and the fishermen—those who bought licenses—have been paying the bill to have beaver protected."

Brant looked meaningfully at Webb.

The boy flushed. He knew that the fees the sportsmen paid to hunt and fish went for other things than the game rangers' salaries!

"Okay." Brant smiled. "I think it's about time the hunters and the fishermen got something back for the money they've put out on beaver." The officer leaned forward to roll a coal out of the fire and up into the bowl of his pipe. He puffed a moment and then flipped the ember out. "You wouldn't want to see beaver over-trapped again, would you?"

"No," Webb admitted. It had only been during the last year or so that his uncle had found beaver numerous enough to make it worthwhile poaching.

"That means supervised trapping. But," added the

ranger, "the beaver in the Colorado River above the dam site—that's another proposition. What do you suppose will happen to the flattails when the dam is finished, and the lake comes up? It will cover this island!"

This was something Webb had not thought about. Brant's questioning created a vision; a lake rising above all these green trees, above the banks of willows and cottonwoods that lined both sides of the river, rising until only the dry canyons and the sheer rock cliffs of the adjoining desert would form the shoreline.

"By golly!" Webb exclaimed, sitting up. "You're right. There'd be nothing for the beaver but cactus and palo verde trees."

"And they can't live on those! The beaver above the dam site are doomed," said the ranger soberly. "It has always been that way—when man makes one of his so-called progressive steps, he kicks wildlife back half a dozen."

They both sat silent, each with his own deep thoughts. Webb looked up into the dark cottonwoods that would be under water in another five years. It saddened him. The trees gave way to an image of Black Mountain rising on the Arizona side of the river, and to the mountains on the Nevada side of the river. These were in rich colors of red, brown and yellow. Webb knew them—bone-dry hills, barren for miles back. A few mountain sheep ranged the ridges and came down to the river for water. There were scattered coveys of Gambel's quail in the canyon. The sheep and the quail could move back as the waters of the lake came up, but not the beaver. They were finished!

This experience with the inquiring game keeper made Webb see hunting, fishing and trapping—and the life he had been living—in a new light. The past four days had filled his mind with long thoughts. As Brant stirred to his feet and untied the rope around his bed, the boy felt a stronger liking for the little man he topped by a full head. He felt a longing to be like him. Later that last night on the river, after the fire had died to ashes, Webb crawled between the blankets with a mind full of new ambitions and exciting hopes.

Even when he woke, just before daylight, his mind picked up where it had left off the night before. Suddenly he wanted to get home, back to his cabin: first he was going to fix his motor, then he would reset the muskrat traps. With the duck and goose hunting season close, he wanted to give Champ a few more lessons in retrieving. Too, he planned to borrow some books he had seen on the shelves in the Murphy home.

Brant woke full of energy. "Let's hurry up and start off. I'm anxious to get back to town. I have things to do if I'm going to get this beaver trapping project rolling before it's too late."

On the way back down the river, Webb remembered how he had felt at the start of the trip. He hoped he would never have to feel that way again, all sick inside.

When they arrived opposite Needles, California, the sun had already set behind the mountains rising to the west. The boy amused himself counting the lights as they came on, flashing like carelessly thrown jewels along the darkening shore. Then they rounded a tule-covered bar and came in sight of the backwater that marked the opening to Webb's own lagoon.

The boy looked ahead, eager for the sight of his cabin. Then he thought he saw the thin, phosphorescent wake of a moving boat coming out of the dark opening. He couldn't be sure, though, and he leaned back to shout, "Shut off the motor."

The thundering died and as their boat slid forward on its own momentum, silence followed. Webb listened and heard the low hum of an outboard coming across the water. Brant heard it, too.

"That boat's coming out of my lagoon!"

Brant started the motor again. Their craft lifted under the full throttle. In a few minutes they were in sight of the other boat. The stranger picked up speed and curved away from the shore, heading downstream and then swinging out to cross the river.

Brant throttled down a moment to shout, "Probably fishermen."

But Webb was disturbed. The man in front had been a much bigger man than the one at the motor! He felt an uneasiness as Brant swung the boat into his lagoon and warped it against the tamarisk log. Webb looked intently at his cabin. It stood quiet and dark, outlined against the trees.

Champ leaped ashore at his master's command. Then he stepped to the log with the tie rope in his hand and dropped a clove hitch over the iron rod embedded there. He pulled the boat close as Brant shut off the gas and made other adjustments on the motor in preparation for leaving it.

"I'll come back in the morning. I'm going home in the truck," said the ranger. "I've had enough of that boat for a while. And say, Webb," added Brant, "tear your motor down first thing and make a list of the parts you need. I'll get them when I go into Kingman tomorrow."

"That'll be swell," answered Webb.

Brant hesitated before climbing into the truck. . . . "Webb, I want you to realize I appreciate your going along. You know your stuff out there in that Slough!"

This made the boy feel good as he picked up his bed-roll and walked toward his cabin. Then he noticed Champ. The dog was sniffing the ground, lifting his head and scenting along the door jamb. The Labrador growled! Webb knew then that the strangers they had met at the mouth of the lagoon had been around his cabin!

He changed his mind quickly and carried his bedroll back up the road and off into the brush. He spread it out in the middle of a thicket and went to sleep with Champ curled at his feet.

7.

WEBB TRAPS BEAVER

It had been a nerve-wracking night and morning for Webb, but now he was feeling better. The game ranger was on his way to Kingman with a list of replacement parts for the broken outboard motor. The boy had finished his own chores, and using the game ranger's boat, had gone around his trapline and reset.

When Webb poled his own boat through a fringe of tules that screened a lagoon bordering the channel of the river, it was well into the afternoon. The hidden lake, completely surrounded by the tall water grass, was deep and wide at one end and the other feathered out into a shoal.

"Drop!" commanded Webb, softly, yet firmly. The Labrador standing on the deck crouched and remained motionless, only his yellow eyes alive. The boy had to grin—the dog knew what was coming. Champ always did when they came to this lagoon.

"It won't be long before we'll have the real thing," he said to the dog as he went about the business of hiding his boat in the tules and simulating a duck-hunting blind.

But as he worked he recalled the things that had upset

69

him. First, the discovery that someone, possibly Bango, had been prowling around his cabin. This had made him leave the cabin and hide his sleeping place, last night. Then, the first thing when he woke up this morning, he had commanded Champ to heel and had circled the cabin. He found the footprints of two men, but oddly enough, nothing had been disturbed.

Mentally, Webb kicked himself again. Just how dumb could he get, he wondered.

On checking the footprints the second time he noticed that one of the men had been wearing cowboy boots. Webb recalled hearing, while he was in jail, that Bango had been a former rodeo bronc rider. Also, that second time over the tracks, he saw where Bango had spit several times, a habit he knew his former tank boss had, because Webb had always been on the floor-mopping detail!

The prickly sensation swept up the back of his neck again, now that he was sure who the visitors of the night before had been.

In his mind, Webb went over the possible reasons why Bango had prowled around his cabin. There seemed to be only one—the tank boss had tried to find out whether or not he had escaped the ordeal in the Slough. Webb knew for certain he would have to avoid meeting Bango, but if he did . . . The boy's eyes dropped to the .22 caliber Remington semiautomatic rifle lying on the worktable. It was a slight weapon of defense in the ordinary man's hands, but not in Webb's. Constant practice had made him deadly accurate with it.

He knew he wasn't going out looking for the tank boss, but he didn't intend to let the brute of a man push him around again either, if they accidentally met.

Webb forced the unpleasant thoughts out of his mind

and he spoke to Champ warningly: "Birds!" The Labrador froze, remaining motionless even to the tip of his quivering tail. Webb, playing the part of a duck hunter, crouched in the boat. He dragged two rag-packed canvas-covered dummy ducks from under the table.

Suddenly he stood up and heaved them high in the air. With a silk-smooth motion, he grabbed the rifle and brought it to his shoulder. A .22 long rifle slug spatted heavily into each falling block before it hit the water.

"Champ!" snapped Webb. The dog rose to his feet, poised, eager. The boy waved toward one of the floating blocks, "Go!" he commanded.

The Labrador leaped to obey, splashing heavily. Webb felt a surge of pride as his dog swam powerfully through the water and retrieved the first block. He leaned down and took it, and sent Champ out for the second. When the Labrador brought the second block, Webb helped him climb to the deck of the boat, patting him and pouring out praise.

"You are a champ, a real winner, boy!"

Webb repeated the same routine then, commanding Champ to lie down. This time he threw one block high and far. As it fell into the tules on the far side of the lagoon, it carried two more slugs from the .22 rifle.

Webb chuckled to the dog, "We're sharp today, fella!"

Then he heaved the second block out over the fringe of tules behind him, out into the channel of the river. He let it bob along on the current a moment or two before he called the Labrador to attention.

"Champ!" The dog rose expectantly. Webb gestured toward the river. "Go!"

The Labrador ran the length of the boat and plunged into the tules and through.

71

The second canvas block had already floated several yards away, but the dog, swimming strongly with all four spread feet, raised himself in the water, saw the floating block and started after it.

Webb watched with admiration. The Labrador, in his estimation, equalled any field dog retriever he'd ever read about, or heard Brant Murphy tell about.

Champ brought the block to Webb and waited to be helped into the boat. Instead, the boy stood up and waved toward the first block he had thrown. It was lying several feet inside the fringe of tules, on the far end of the lagoon.

"Go!" Champ swam in the direction indicated.

Webb stood on the deck to watch, and saw that the Labrador's course was taking him several yards to the left of the block, which was well hidden from the swimming dog's sight. Webb waited until Champ had almost reached the tules, then he whistled, a single, sharp blast. The dog stopped and turned in the water, watching his master. Webb waved his arm to the right. Champ turned and swam at right angles to his first course.

When Champ was in direct line with the block, Webb whistled again, stopping the dog, then sent him straight into the tules toward the block. In a few minutes the Labrador reappeared, the block in his mouth, sprang into the water and swam toward the boat.

"Gee!" exclaimed Webb, almost to himself, but mostly to the dog as he helped the dripping animal onto the deck, "We'll have to show that to Brant some time—that's a grandstand retrieve!" Then he added wistfully, "I wish I had papers on you, Champ, so we could enter some real field trials."

The dog shook the water from his heavy coat and

wagged his tail in response to the praise and the lavish petting, as Webb dried him with a gunny sack.

"Got your full growth now, haven't you, pup?" said Webb, hefting the muscular dog. "You'll weigh well up there, seventy-five or eighty pounds, I'll bet!" He knew the retriever was bigger than most of his breed, and more powerful. He knew, too, that Champ was a first-class hunter.

Webb repeated Champ's training sessions every afternoon during the next few days, whenever he had finished the work involved with his muskrat trapping.

Late one afternoon, four days after Brant had left, as Webb swung into his lagoon, he knew he had visitors even before he came in sight of the wharf. Champ gave him warning. The boy pulled his rifle within easy, quick reach.

The precaution was unwarranted for it was the game ranger standing on the tamarisk log. Another man was up on the bank, a stranger to Webb.

"Hi!" greeted the boy with a sigh of relief as Brant caught the gliding boat.

"Webb," said the ranger, his brown eyes crinkling and squinting against the westering sun, "jump out and meet Tom Jesson."

"Howdy," grunted the stranger.

Webb shook hands with the man as they sized each other up. Jesson was an outdoorsman. Something about his clothes, his hat, the way he wore them and his handshake told Webb this.

The older man silently looked the boy up and down with his one bright blue eye—the other was sightless. Webb felt an instinctive liking for the taciturn fellow.

Brant broke the silence. "I've got a lot of talking to do with you two. Webb, can we use your cabin?"

"Sure thing," answered Webb, unlocking the door. He lit the gasoline lamp and offered Jesson the only chair. The ranger took the stool and Webb perched himself on the edge of the bunk, after lighting the stove and setting water on for coffee.

Brant leaned forward, rubbing his hands. "The beaver trapping project is for sure, Webb. The Commission authorized us to start as soon as we can get outfitted."

"Us? We?" questioned Webb, disappointment sweeping across his face. "It's a state trapping project then . . . for state-hired trappers?"

Brant grinned, saying, "Yes, if that's what you and Tom want to call yourselves."

74

Webb looked at the older man. Tom stared back silently.
"You mean, I—I'm to be a beaver trapper?"

Brant nodded.

"Sayin' so don't make it so," pronounced Tom Jesson
drily. "But you look like you might have the makin's, Boy.
If you know how to work, you might be a beaver trapper
afore this is over."

Brant looked at Tom and laughed, then he hastily went
on to explain. "We've got it worked out, except for the
details, Webb. The state game department will pay you
five dollars for every cured pelt, and furnish you with
everything except your bed and food. Tom helped me work
it out. We're having some pontoons made now . . . flat-
bottom boats with plywood decks . . . two of them. You
can bolt them together and set your tent up on them,
with plenty of room for everything else: cots, stoves, tables
. . . well, everything you need for a good camp. The beauty
of the thing is we can float it anywhere . . . tow it with a
twenty-two motor."

Brant leaned forward toward the boy. "Incidentally,
Webb, we'll furnish you with a new Johnson or Evinrude
motor, whichever you prefer, and a river boat, that is, if
you want to get in on this deal."

Webb sat silent, trying to think what this would mean
to him. The ranger went on.

"Tom here, will work with you. You can throw in together, or each trap for himself. Tom says he'd like to
work with you, share and share alike. He feels he's a little
old to run a trapline, and since you know the Slough and
the river, he'll teach you how to trap beaver and then settle
down and keep camp, repair trapping equipment and do
most of the skinning and stretching. How about it?"

Webb agreed and the trio went on to finish planning.

As the dusk deepened, the boy rose and busied himself at the stove. Soon the odor of coffee filled the cabin. Webb poured mugs of the steaming brew for each and passed the heavy cups around.

Tom took an experimental sip and smacked his lips. "Man's coffee, all right," he nodded approvingly, his raised eyebrows expressing the surprise he wouldn't admit.

Brant stood up and put a hand on Webb's shoulder. "He'll make you a hand, Tom. A good hand!"

After Brant and Tom left that night Webb was a long time going to sleep. Things were bound to be better for him, because if beaver could be caught, he'd catch them. And, at five dollars . . .

For the first time in his life Webb felt as if he had a real goal to strive for . . . something that could mean . . .

8

THE THREAT OF BANGO

As Webb knelt on the deck of the pontoons and steadied the ranger's craft, Brant Murphy carefully stepped into the center of the boat and walked to the stern, where he sat down.

"She's all yours, boys. The fate of Arizona's first beaver management program is in your capable hands," he said. Then, with a chuckle, he added, "High-sounding speech, wasn't it? But that about says it. It's up to you fellows now."

All at once, in spite of the ranger's joking, Webb realized that the project meant more to Brant than just the successful trapping and skinning of beaver.

Tom looked up from the pile of traps he was sorting on the deck of the float. "We'll have a stack of beaver pelts for you when you come back—don't worry."

Brant looked up at Webb and smiled warmly, with a flash of gold. "Okay, turn me loose."

As the boat drifted away on the current, the ranger lifted both his hands above his head and clasped them together in the manner of a boxer shaking hands with the cheering crowd. Webb knew the gesture was for him, that Brant was depending a lot on him for the success of the venture. Then the ranger started his motor and disappeared among the tules.

Tom jerked Webb back to reality. "What d'you say we make some sets and get Murphy's beaver management program rolling?"

"That's for me!" exclaimed Webb, jumping into action. They had been more than a week in preparation for trapping beaver, and the delay had created both impatience and eagerness in the boy. In that time he had heard Tom tell of experiences trapping beaver throughout the Northwest, all the way from Michigan to Alaska and back again. He was looking forward to seeing how Tom would make his sets. Now, traps, weights, wire and various other tools went into Webb's new boat. Tom sat in the front and Webb commanded Champ to sit on the worktable. Then he started the motor.

After a few minutes of traveling the waterways through the clumps of tules, Webb ran to an island in the Slough. The brush there showed signs of beaver-cuttings. The bank was marked with slides and the air was heavy with the sweet scent of the animal.

"That looks like a good place, Tom. What do you think?"

The old man looked a moment, then said tersely, "It'll do." He pulled on his hip boots, hitching them to his belt. "Run her nose into the bank, hold her and hand me the tools . . . the shovel first."

Webb watched the older man take a shovelful of mud from under the water, about eighteen inches from the bank, and directly under a slide that showed use.

"Now a stake and the axe," commanded Tom.

The old trapper drove the stake into the bank close to
the shelf, pounding it down until the top was under water
and out of sight.

Webb recognized it as the same kind of set that the
poachers had made; he wondered where Bango was now.
But Tom interrupted his thoughts.

"As soon's we catch a beaver, we'll have some castors
. . . then I'll show you how's to make a set usin' scent.
It's the best kind!"

Standing hip-deep in water, Tom leaned over the edge
of the boat and stripped off about eight feet of smooth
wire from a coil. One end of this wire he fastened to the
stake. The other he fed through a hole drilled through

79

the shorter end of a piece of L-shaped steel, of which he had many. He attached a trap by its chain to the longer arm of the L.

Webb saw that it would serve the same purpose as the locking device he had seen on the poacher's set—only Tom's was better, because it was simpler.

"You've got to have this put on the wire right," explained the trapper, "or it won't work. The long end has to point away from the stake, so as it can slide down the wire."

Tom demonstrated by pulling on the trap chain and sliding the device along the wire, then he reversed the direction of pull and the simple device jammed.

The old trapper went on, "A beaver'll dive the minute it feels a trap, an' this," he said, sliding the L forward, "will follow him down." Tom looked up. "But when he comes up or tries to get back on the bank, it'll jam, an' drown him, quick!"

Webb thought he knew why the quick finish was the most practical, as well as the most humane way, even before the trapper went on with his explanations.

"Killing a beaver quick makes sense a lot of ways. First, he's got a trap on his foot and it's hurtin'. For another, if he has time, he'll spin in the water an' twist his foot off. This catch is good for another reason—it'll hold him down where other beaver can't get at him. Funny thing amongst beaver, if a boar beaver gets caught in a trap and gets out on the bank, an' another one comes along, it'll cut him all to pieces killin' him. An' that sure enough ruins a nice pelt."

The old man frowned and bent to his work. "Been runnin' off my mouth so much I'm forgettin' to finish the set."

He turned then and Webb saw him attach a heavy piece

of scrap iron to the loose end of the wire, which he threw out into the deep water, stretching the wire from the stake.

Webb offered the old trapper a clamp for depressing the spring, but Tom refused it. Instead, he placed the trap on his thigh, pushed the spring down with his gnarled but muscular hands and set the trap. He looked up, his single blue eye bright from the effort, and wagged his head.

"When you can set a number four with your bare hands, you'll be a beaver trapper!"

Webb made the rest of the sets that day, and that evening Tom said, "Remember, make your sets good, an' you'll catch beaver."

The following morning, the two were out on the water at sunup. Tom had roused Webb up in the early dark with, "When you're trappin' beaver, you work from 'can-see t' can't-see.'"

They found a beaver in the first set, the one Tom had made.

As the animal bobbed to the surface when the trapper pulled up the weight, he said, "I don't like trappin' a slide. You catch too many little ones."

He then partially skinned out the hind legs and removed the castors, which, Webb could see, were each about the size of a small hen's egg.

"Now I'll make a stink set," said Tom, holding up the musk glands. "Let's find a run."

They had to partially circle the little island before they found a bank worn smooth with the passing of beaver feet, and here Webb nosed the boat into the bank. While he held the craft in position, the older trapper made the set.

First he took several shovelfuls of mud from under the water and piled them up on the bank at the water's edge.

Then he fashioned an underwater shelf upon which he set the trap. The stake, the wire and the weight were employed in the same way as in the first set he had shown Webb.

"You put the trap deeper in this one, an' about eighteen inches out from the bank. A beaver'll swim up to this 'stink mound' I'm makin' an' put his front feet on the bank an' float. He'll let his hind feet sag down into the trap—that's where you want to catch a big beaver, by his hind foot."

As the old man finished, he splashed water up on the mound to wash away any possible man-smell, even though he hadn't been on shore. Then he carefully squeezed the contents of one of the fresh castors on the top of the mound.

After Tom had climbed into the boat, Webb backed the craft away.

"This is the best set for beaver. If your lock is workin' right and your weight's heavy enough to hold 'em down, you'll hold nineteen out o' twenty beaver that springs your trap."

Tom scooted around in his seat so that he could face Webb. "Another thing that's good about a stink set is this—most beaver you catch will be 'blankets,' big ones. The little ones'll swim right over a trap baited with scent. It makes sense, you catch the old beaver an' you leave the small ones for next trappin' season."

Webb looked at the man with silent wonder. Somehow, this old outdoorsman had gotten the same slant on hunting, fishing and trapping that Brant Murphy had learned while working for the game department. It was something to think about, the boy decided.

The thoughtful look on Webb's face registered with Tom, and he went on, "A trapper can catch himself out of business if he takes ever'thing." The old man cocked his head, turning it slightly so as to bring Webb under the full sight of his one eye. "If you learn that one rule about beaver trappin', take some and leave some, there'll always be beaver to catch."

For the next week Webb was setting and running traps from daylight to dark. He found it harder work than muskrat trapping, because each set had to be made with elaborate preparations. Tom insisted on that, and even went with him several times to inspect the sets the boy had made. But the rewards for the hard work were greater. Webb was catching as many as ten beaver a day, and eight out of ten of the furbearers measured up to blankets.

However, the greatest of the rewards came at the end of the week when the old trapper announced in an elaborately offhand way, "You're doin' all right—we've got seventy-three pelts curin'."

The following day, Webb came in with eighteen beaver, the biggest catch he had made.

Tom couldn't quite hold his pose of sour-puss as he prepared to skin them. He smiled a little in a rusty way. "That's ten a day—or twenty-five dollars a day—for each of us. Good money, but I wish'd we was trappin' for ourselves."

"Why?" asked Webb.

"These blankets'll bring thirty dollars or better, the dark ones. The light ones—the gray ones—won't go so good."

"Like this silvery-colored one?" asked Webb, picking up a beaver and tossing it up into the cradle that Tom had made to ease the job of skinning.

"Yeah, the off-colored ones," grunted the trapper, stroking his skinning knife on a pocket stone as he approached.

Suddenly the older man leaned forward and peered closely at one of the beaver's hind feet.

"This beaver's been in another trap besides yours . . . not more'n three days ago. He twisted out of it, an' lost that toe."

Webb looked closely at the still raw stump, something he had taken more or less for granted, without giving thought to it.

"What makes you think it was a trap?" he asked.

Tom Jesson appeared to be almost insulted as he looked across the beaver at Webb. It was a moment before he answered a bit tartly, "I was catching beaver when your mama was singin' you to sleep with, 'Your Daddy's gone a-huntin' to catch a little rabbit skin, to wrap our Baby Buntin' in!' I say there's a poacher trappin' the Slough."

Webb swallowed hard. He felt goose pimples forming on his neck and arms.

Bango was back!

9

THE CONTRABANDERS OFFER A DEAL

All during that morning Webb had a feeling of anxiety. Even the .22 autoloader rifle lying on the worktable was of little comfort. Time after time he caught himself standing motionless in the boat, listening for the putting of a strange motor in the Slough. He wished his own motor were silent as he shut it off again and the boat glided up the lagoon.

The Labrador, standing spraddle-legged on the deck, seemed to sense his master's nervousness and whined. Webb looked at the dog, glistening yellow and golden in the morning sun, rope-like muscles bulging like poorly made splices under the skin.

"Gee, Champ," he said softly, "I'd really be spooky if you weren't along."

The dog jumped across the front well onto the table spanning the middle of the boat, and walked gingerly among the beaver carcasses to his master. As Webb affectionately scratched his ears the retriever made little grunts of pleasure. The boy idly turned the left one inside out and looked at the peculiar arrangement of tattooed dots on the inside, five of them in a ragged geometric design. Webb had discovered the markings the fall before when Champ had got a foxtail in his ear. Now again he wondered about the dots, patted Champ's sides, pushed him back. He picked up the paddle to swerve the gliding boat into the bank where the last trap was set.

The huge silvery beaver that bobbed to the surface when Webb pulled up the set interrupted his thoughts about the dog. He gave a soft, almost soundless whistle when he saw that the beaver had a pegged leg. The partially-healed stump was still raw.

A prickly sensation crawled up the back of his neck, the same kind he had felt the afternoon before, when he thought of Bango. He was scared. He knew it. He didn't try to kid himself. Very hurriedly he reset the trap and started the motor.

As he made a fast run back to camp he half expected the tank boss' boat to pop out of every tule-screened waterway. It was with a distinct feeling of relief that he came in sight of the pontoons anchored at the head of the long, tule-covered island.

Thinking of Bango had so occupied Webb's mind that he'd forgotten entirely that this was the game ranger's day to visit their camp, bring supplies and pick up the cured beaver pelts. It wasn't until he saw Brant's boat that he remembered, and then, quite suddenly and unexpectedly, a thought crept into his mind.

Tom and Brant were busy stacking cured beaver pelts like huge chips in the officer's boat. They didn't look up until Webb shut off his motor and coasted into the bank.

"Hi!" greeted Brant, and without pausing for Webb to reply he said, "You fellows are really making a good catch!"

86

As the prow of Webb's boat scraped up on the bank he picked up the three-legged beaver and tossed it ashore at Tom's feet.

"Another light one," commented the trapper disgustedly. Then Tom saw the raw stump. "Another peg! That poacher again!"

Webb watched silently as Brant Murphy dropped to his knees to examine the beaver with Tom.

"Twisted loose . . . from a trap . . . not more'n three or four days ago," said Tom flatly. "Webb, did you lose any lately? This makes two pegs you've caught!"

"Had a few sprung since we started," replied Webb, "but I haven't held any feet."

Webb was conscious of Brant's questioning gaze. The ranger turned to Tom. "What do you mean?"

"Webb's caught two beaver that've been in traps before," answered Tom tersely.

"Traps set by poachers?"

"Not Webb's. Not if he sets 'm the way I showed him. He'll drown every one he gits aholt of."

Webb, still in the boat, looked up at Brant. The expression on the ranger's face told the boy that the officer was thinking of the same thing—of that day in the channel when Webb had told of his first encounter with the poachers, when Brant had doubted his story!

"Webb, you'll remember I told you it would all come out in time," the ranger said, nodding in agreement with his own statement. "I'm mighty glad it has—I'm glad you were leveling with me that time!"

Tom looked up, completely puzzled at what had been said.

Brant, noticing the older man's bewilderment, hastened to explain, "Webb and I had a little misunderstanding on the survey, Tom. He was right in what he told me, and I doubted him at the time. Now I'm sorry I didn't believe him." The ranger paused a moment, as though he were going to say something else, then suddenly moved away, saying briskly, "I've got to get loaded and back to my place with these furs before dark, or somebody might try to hijack them." He laughed at his own statement, then, thinking of what he'd said, he added, "Say, what am I laughing for? It could happen at that!"

"You're danged right it could," grunted Tom, picking up a stack of beaver pelts. "There's many a man has had his camp robbed of beaver!"

Webb jumped out and helped with the labors. They were finished quickly and Brant stepped into his boat to leave. He started to crank the motor, then stopped and turned to the two on shore.

"I was just thinking, you fellows haven't had any fun for nearly three weeks. The camp's cleaned out of cured pelts, so you two could run over to Needles and take in a show and come back in the morning. Maybe buy some magazines to read in camp."

Tom spoke up quickly. "Not me, I'll sit on the camp. But Webb might like to go."

Webb shook his head ruefully. "Gosh, I'd like to go, but I haven't enough money."

Brant grinned. "I can fix that, easy! Here's a ten." The ranger waved Webb's protest down. "Pay me back out of your first pay check from the state . . . and have a good time. You've earned it."

Webb and Tom watched the officer's boat weave through the tules and finally disappear from sight.

Tom's good eye gleamed warmly as he finally turned. "Pretty nice feller, that Brant!"

Webb had to agree. He could feel the new ten-dollar bill, stiff and crisp, clutched in his hand. It made him think of the many things he could do, now that he had a little money of his own.

"You better git scootin', Webb, or they'll be turnin' out the lights and rollin' up the sidewalks before you git there. You could bring me a few things, and I'll take care of your dog for you."

Webb smiled and shook his head. "Thanks, Tom, I'll get your things, but I want to take Champ. He's going to get a couple cans of that specially-prepared dog food out of this, huh, ol' boy?" He knelt for a moment, affectionately rubbing his knuckles along the dog's backbone, scratching him, and both Webb and Tom laughed when Champ's hind leg began to kick at the stimulus.

Thirty minutes later, Webb was threading his boat through the waterways, headed west. He could see the smoke from the railroad terminal rising over the tules. He sang aloud and once whistled. The idea of an evening in town was like Christmas Eve had been when he was a kid.

It was late afternoon when Webb swung his boat into the Needles boat landing. The old man in charge greeted him.

"Hi, young fellow! How's the beaver trapping going?"

Webb had known Rudy MacDonald most of his life, at least since he and his Uncle Jake had lived in the Slough, for they had often docked here when buying their few groceries.

Webb was friendly, but he was curious, too. "It's going fine. Been catching about ten a day . . . but how did you know we were trapping beaver?"

"That sort of news travels fast. A fellow told me Arizona

89

and California must o' worked out some kind of a deal, huh?"

Webb shook his head. "I don't know. I'm working for the state . . . Arizona. Say, Mac, can I moor my boat?" Webb grinned. "I'll pay for it this time! I'm earning money now. . . . And gas it up too, will you?"

"Sure will. Glad to hear you finally got hold of something. Beaver ought to sell real high."

Webb was about to explain the arrangement under which he was working, then thought better of it. He was surprised that he was just a little ashamed of what he was doing, or rather how he was doing it.

MacDonald disappeared in his office, and came out almost immediately with a slip of paper.

"That reminds me. There's a fellow darned interested in your beaver trapping. He left me this number for me to call in case you ever docked over here. Said he wanted to talk to you. Where you going to stay, Webb?"

"I don't know," replied Webb, cautious but instantly curious. "Who was it? What did he want?"

MacDonald shook his head. "He and another fellow rented a boat a couple of times last week. That's all I know. Say, why don't you stay at the Green Lantern Motel—I'll call and reserve a room for you there." The dock manager left then to go into his office.

Webb stood undecided a minute. He wanted to ask more questions, but he remembered all the things he had to do before the stores closed, so he hurried into town, commanding Champ to stay at his heels.

Here and there he ran into people he knew. He would have liked to stop and talk, but he pressed on, accumulating things and checking them off the list he and Tom had prepared.

It was almost seven o'clock when he checked in at the Green Lantern, locked Champ in the room and hurried to the movie. It was a western, about cattle ranching. Webb liked it, for ranch life would be his choice if he couldn't do something like he was doing now. But after the show he knew punching cattle could not compare with his recent experiences; this he told himself with conviction as he hurried back to the motel.

It was almost eleven o'clock when he reached his room. He unlocked the door and then took Champ for a short walk. The Labrador investigated all the building corners and trees along the walk.

"You're glad to get in and meet your friends, too, huh, Champ?" Webb chuckled.

Dogs, like beaver, must have some sort of registry, he decided.

Finally he called Champ and they went back to his room at the motel. As he unlocked the door, a man crossed the street behind him, coming toward him.

"You Webb Dodge?"

"Yes, I am," replied Webb, stepping back.

"I've been waiting for you. MacDonald down at the dock called me. That will explain it to you."

"Oh," said Webb, instantly on the alert. "You're the fellow that wants to see me." He opened the door, but the man waved him through first.

"Yeah, want to talk to you." The man took off his hat and sat down in the only chair in the room. Webb sat on the bed, after commanding Champ to lie down.

The stranger smoothed his black hair. He leaned to one side, took a pack of cigarettes from his coat's side pocket and smiled—smiled like a coyote, thought Webb, as he refused the offered smoke.

"Never had enough money to acquire the habit."

Webb noticed the gold ring and the expensive wrist watch as the other lit a cigarette. The jewelry seemed to fit, the cigarettes were oval and cork-tipped.

Webb felt uncomfortable as the man studied him with half-closed eyes through the up-drifting smoke. Finally the stranger spoke. "How's the beaver trapping?"

"Fine," replied Webb, wondering immediately how the man knew.

"Webb," said the man matter of factly and as though nothing ever surprised him, "I figure you're a pretty smart kid, so I'm going to put it to you straight." Then he paused, watching impassively.

Webb squirmed uneasily. Then he felt his face freeze into a set smile. He wasn't going to show it, but curiosity consumed him. He wanted to know what the man had on his mind.

"Okay, here it is. I know your deal. You're trapping beaver for Arizona and California—at five bucks a pelt. Right? The states are splitting the expenses, and taking all the sale money. Right?"

Webb was surprised. The man knew all the details, so he nodded confirmation.

Before speaking again, the man leaned forward, opening the smooth palm of his left hand, and poked it with a manicured nail on a slender forefinger.

"The states are creaming off on your deal, and giving you skimmed milk. Five bucks!" He snorted in disgust. "Beaver are selling for thirty to forty bucks, *and* they're only cutting you in for five. I'll double that." Then he pulled out a packet of bills, folded once and held by a gold clip. As he riffled them, Webb could see they were mostly twenty-dollar bills.

The man took a slow drag on his cigarette, letting the smoke curl out of his mouth as he watched Webb's reaction.

"I'll give you a straight ten bucks a pelt, large or medium," He paused, looking ceilingward, appearing to be thinking. "That's a lot of dough, Kid! And I'll pay you for ten—your first ten—right now!"

Webb watched fascinated at the sight of so much money and at the slow, deliberate separating of five twenty-dollar bills.

"That's an easy hundred! And a clean deal! This'll be the only time you'll ever see me or talk to me. All you have to do is choose an island in the Slough, leave the pelts there and we'll have a man pick 'em up. You leave the pelts, and we'll leave the money."

The man looked directly at Webb, eyes cold and hard as obsidian. They reminded the boy of the eyes of a hunting animal, crouched to pounce.

"Just name the place, and you've got yourself a deal," the man urged in low tones, holding out the five twenty-dollar bills, spread like a hand of cards.

Webb hesitated, trying to catch up with his tumbling thoughts, and to control his hands that wanted to reach out and take the money.

"Heard you just got out of a jam, with your uncle. That was a bum operation, but this is a clean deal. Where do we pick up the skins?"

Webb looked at the money. One hundred dollars! He could not remember having seen that much at one time before. It could be his—to buy a new boat, a new motor. But the man's last words reminded him of the trouble he had been in . . . and of his obligation to Brant. He couldn't cross the game ranger. Money or not, his loyalty was with Brant Murphy. He stood up slowly.

"No. I guess . . . I guess not. I can't make a deal."

The man looked at Webb calculatingly, his eyes narrowing.

Licking his lips, he smiled wetly. "I knew you were smart! You speak my language. Okay, fifteen bucks," he said, peeling off two more twenties and a ten. Fifty more! "We'll leave it for the first ten pelts."

Webb had to grip himself hard. He knew he'd have to hurry before he weakened. "You've got me wrong. You can't buy in on this."

Again the man looked at Webb, raising his eyebrows and squinting sidewise.

"I catch. You've got a connection."

Webb shook his head. "These beaver pelts aren't for sale, except through the game department."

The man pinched his thin lips together and spoke impatiently, as if reasoning with a not-too-bright child. "I'm offering you three times what you're getting now. Don't be so dumb!"

The implied insult was what clinched the wavering boy into action. Nothing made him madder than to have his intelligence slighted. He stepped forward, then turned and jerked the door open. The man saw Webb's rising anger. Too, the dog had raised his head at the mounting voices and the tension.

"Okay, okay. No hard feelings. You might change your mind when you hear how much they're getting for beaver pelts. So, if you want to cut yourself a better deal, leave a note with MacDonald down at the dock. Just put 'Jerry' on the envelope, and seal it." The man stopped in front of the mirror by the door and carefully adjusted his hat at just the right angle.

Without turning, he said, "Think it over, Webb. But remember, the longer you wait, the more money you'll lose. Beaver are only prime for a couple of months."

Then he stepped outside, unhurried and confident, while Webb, hand clenched on the door knob, watched him go. Champ growled a little, deep in his throat.

10

THE FIRE ON THE ISLAND

It was just breaking day when Webb steered the boat, which he was running at half-speed, out from behind the breakwater and onto the main channel of the river. There he shut off the motor, to drift for a moment. The wind was blowing cold out of the north, and the boy stood up, shivering. But it felt good, pushing against the cold, clean wind.

He had spent an almost sleepless night, with a continuous half-dream, half-fantasy playing through his mind. He couldn't help but think of all the money he had been offered. He'd tried to think of something else, but the size of the man's offer kept coming back. When you'd been poor all your life . . .

Unconsciously, he now became aware of a thin, wavering line crossing the lightening sky. Faintly—ever so faintly —he heard the cackling call of the geese,

"Cad-dia-lac-lac! Cad-dia-lac-lac!"

He listened hard, thinking for a moment he heard the chug of an outboard motor across the river, whispering as

it hurried down the channel. But he dismissed the idea. It was too early for anyone else to be out.

Before starting his motor again, he reached under the seat and pulled out a three-foot length of polished wood that had once been a shovel handle. One end was tapered to fit the tiller. He made it secure, then he started the motor and stood up in the stern, balancing easily, steering with the extension.

Webb knew the Colorado, a treacherous waterway, filled with constantly-shifting sandbars. Standing in a boat was one of the cardinal sins of boating, he knew, but these were not normal circumstances, and the danger of running onto a sandbar was greater than that of capsizing.

Ahead, he saw a riffling which he knew marked a shoal. He swung upstream to go above the gilhooly, then pushed out onto the main sweep of the river. Giving the outboard full throttle, he skimmed across toward the tule-lined edge of the Slough.

Webb noticed that the wind had turned and was building; he could feel it on his back, and was thankful it was behind him. With his heavy load, the current of the river was enough to buck. He stayed close to the tule-fringed edge of the Slough, swinging in and out as he followed the weaving contour of the shoreline.

Soon he swerved into a break, the opening to a hidden waterway he knew, a boat path that would take him to the island where he and Tom were camped. Here he had shelter from the full force of the cold wind, which was getting stronger.

Webb came to a wide place and shut off his motor. He wanted to listen to the wind soughing in the tall river grass. It always gave him a thrill—the fall wind rustling the dead tules, the scudding clouds, low-flying ducks that were always on the wing in the early morning.

A triple of teal flashed over. Champ watched, his eyes like amber lights and his powerful body taut.

"Greenwing," Webb breathed, raising an imaginary shotgun. "We'd get a double there, wouldn't we, Champ?" The retriever wagged his tail, watched the ducks wing out of sight. A cat's-paw of wind traced a V on the water near the boat.

Webb inhaled the cold air and felt good. The events of the morning had cleared his mind, and he remembered he had work to do.

Soon he came to a long, straight channel which opened in front of him. At the far end he could just catch a glimpse of the island he and Tom were using for their base camp.

The boy felt a laugh rising in his chest. Maybe . . . just maybe . . . he'd catch his old partner in bed and have a chance to give him the hurrah. By now Webb knew Tom was not nearly as sour as he liked to appear.

But as the boy looked through the narrow gap between

the rows of tules, he caught a movement in the shadows. A pinpoint of light leaped into a flashing knife of flame. Startled, he stared as the one fiery sword became many. The morning wind caught the flames and swept them ahead; it was as if the fire were fed by gasoline.

Webb shoved the throttle over. His boat leaped through the narrow opening as he ducked the whipping and cutting blades of tule. Then suddenly there was another boat silhouetted against the light of the fire. He caught a shape of a man, a big man, crouched in the stern. As he looked, the strange boat accelerated and disappeared down a branching waterway which led out to the river.

The roaring blaze, creating its own draft, was flaring through the tops of the tinder-dry tules.

Then the sight of an empty gas can bobbing toward him on the water registered in the boy's mind, and things began to add up. Someone was trying to burn him and Tom out! Even now, the rising wind would be fanning the fire ahead, toward the trapper's camp on the end of the island. It was too late to chase after the other boat, but Webb didn't waste any more time wondering what to do. He knew!

Catching Tom in bed wasn't any joke now! He hoped, with a dry mouth, that the old trapper was up and would see the fire coming. He remembered the raw beaver pelts —almost twenty of them—still curing! And the cans of gasoline and oil mixture—the outboard motor fuel—stacked a little way from camp!

He had to get there—in a hurry!

Webb threw his caution overboard and sent his boat twisting like a live thing through the narrow waterways. Every time he missed a log or a tule stump by the thickness of a coat of paint he felt the sharp grasp of fear, but he didn't slacken his speed. He just had to get there in time!

The fast-moving front of flames was now behind him, as he skirted the island. A coot, beating its wings frantically, rose out of the blaze, flew over him and plummeted into the water. As he roared past the fallen bird, Webb could see the singed wing and tail feathers.

Anger crowded out other emotions, even fear, as the boy crouched in the stern, grimly picking a course for the thundering boat which twisted tortuously under his guiding hand. He didn't dare look back at the fire, but the heavy pall of smoke told him it was close behind.

Ahead, the channel widened to the open water surrounding the head of the island. He slurred the boat around, and there was the camp—the tent on the float, anchored to the shore by two long ropes.

Webb shut the motor off at just the right instant, allowing himself enough momentum to coast right up to the side of the pontoons.

Champ leaped, barking excitedly as Tom appeared in the door of the tent, barefooted and in his underwear.

The wake created by the speeding boat caught up as the craft slowed, lifting it high. Webb jumped for the deck of the pontoons, the tie-rope in his hand.

"We've got to get everything off the island," he yelled. "Somebody has fired the tules!" Tom looked as Webb waved toward the rising smoke and flames now bearing down on the camp. The old man leaped to the island and started throwing gear onto the deck.

Webb ran to the stretched and drying pelts hanging on the rack. He grabbed armfuls of the precious furs and stacked them on the float, piling them like huge platters.

Both trappers worked in silent but frenzied desperation. Champ, excited by the activity, barked nervously until

*He didn't dare look back at the fire, but the heavy pall of
smoke told him it was close behind*

Webb commanded him into the boat and to silence.

The fire was now so close they could feel its hot breath. Bits of flaming tules, whipped up by the blaze-created draft and caught by wind, dropped about them, starting little fires closer by.

Finally the last of the gear was on the float.

Webb leaped into the boat, drawing the sheath knife at his belt as he jumped and slashing the tie-rope. He started the motor and curved upstream above the pontoon. Then he backed swiftly and skillfully to the prow of the barge and cut the anchoring rope. He took the free end and snaked it under the boat seat and up, tying a half-hitch. Tom saw what he was doing, and cut the rope which anchored the stern.

The motor thundered as it labored forward. Webb knew that if he could get the prow of the plywood pontoons away from the bank, he might be able to spin the barge off. But the pressing river current held it tight.

The boat wallowed and strained. Water churned up under the thrust of the propeller. The loaded barge did not move.

Webb began to feel a sickening despair, but he held the throttle wide open and gritted his teeth. He heard a splash and turned in time to see Tom jump into the water between the pontoon and the island. Flames licked greedily at the tules near the old man's back. Webb watched, marveling at his partner's courage. Tom had his head down between his arms, shielding the tender skin of his face from the fierce heat. He heaved and heaved against the resisting barge. Gradually, under the combined pull of the motor and Tom's pushing, the big float began to move!

The gap between the pontoons and the island widened.

The current of the river swept in behind, and the barge turned faster.

At last it floated free!

Webb looked back. The exhausted trapper hung at arm's length from the edge of the pontoons, his body trailing in the cold water.

The outboard churned and the boat lurched on the taut rope as Webb held the throttle on full. He looked back again to see that Tom had revived and was hanging on with one hand, his one good eye gleaming triumphantly up at Webb. Tom gave a cracked cheer and shook his fist at the flaming tules.

Then Webb realized, with a swelling pride, that they had won the fight to save the camp.

Jockeying the boat and the trailing barge across the channel and away from the burning island, Webb brought the whole outfit up against another stand of tules, where the current caught and held it. He shut off the motor and jumped back on the deck of the barge, where he knelt down and helped the old man on board.

"I'll be double-danged," Tom said caustically when he had his breath. "That sure happened fast!"

"You can say that again," Webb agreed, clenching his teeth and looking back at the island. The upper end was now aflame. The rack that had held the beaver pelts was burning through and falling down. On the lower part of the island, which had already burned over, only a scattering of flames flickered, and an occasional tree was still flaring. But for their efforts, the beaver-trapping camp would now be a mass of flames.

"That was a sure-enough flash fire, if I ever saw one," said Tom. "How'd it start?"

Webb was about to answer when he heard the regular

pulsing of an outboard motor. He cocked his head and opened his mouth, to hear better. The boat was running up the main channel of the river, behind the tules which screened the edge of the Slough. It was coming closer. In a few minutes the craft rounded a clump of tules.

Webb relaxed, limp with relief; it was Brant.

"What happened?" he called.

"Somebody set the tules on fire," answered Webb.

"No!"

"That's right. I saw them . . . him . . . leave as I came across from Needles this morning." Webb went on to tell about the floating gas can.

"Have any idea who it was?" the ranger asked, looking at him sharply.

Webb hesitated. "I never saw his face."

Brant frowned and pursed his lips, then chugged one balled fist into the open palm of his other hand. "Those birds are playing rough."

"I'd say they were trying to scare us out of the Slough," said Tom with a fighting gleam in his bright blue eye. "They want this beaver trapping to theirselves."

"That's about it," agreed Brant.

"Well, I'm not bluffing out," commented Tom flatly.

The wiry old man had now fully recovered from his strenuous experience, and was standing on the barge deck in his bare feet. He turned to Webb.

"Yep, I'm stayin'. How about you?"

"I was here before they came, and I think I'll be here when they're gone," Webb answered quietly. His eyes narrowed as he spoke. He thought of Bango, the tank boss.

Brant's slow smile held a mixture of surprise and approval as he asked the next question.

"But what are you going to do now? Move? Where?"

"I'd say they were trying to scare us out of the Slough,"
said Tom with a fighting gleam in his bright blue eye

"Tom," Webb turned to the older man, "what about moving camp to the upper end of the Slough? We've taken the best beaver out of here, and we've got to trap that end anyway, before we move upriver."

"That's a good idea," agreed Brant as Tom nodded reflectively. The game ranger went on, looking out of the corners of his eyes at Webb, "It's up close to the sandbars, too, and the duck and goose shooting is opening up in a couple of weeks. That's right, isn't it, Webb?" Then he laughed, because he could see that he had read the boy's mind correctly.

They agreed to move their camp to the Arizona bank of the river, above the Slough.

"I know just the place—under some old cottonwood trees," Webb said. "We can anchor the pontoons next to the bank, and there's plenty of wood for campfires every night."

11

THE SILVER BEAVER TOP THE MARKET

Webb wakened before daylight. He rolled over and opened his eyes, feeling a little sick. Then he remembered —the dream. For once he'd had all the money he needed for good food, clothes, motorboats, guns, a satisfactory place to live in . . . the money had come from pelts he had smuggled . . . stolen . . . and sold to the contraband fur buyers. Still under its golden spell though he was, the boy felt ashamed of the dream.

He moved uneasily, put his hands behind his head and thought of the well-dressed stranger in Needles. He wondered sometimes if he had been too hasty in turning down the stranger's offer. Money . . . lots of money . . . would be nice to have. You'd never have that hungry, lost feeling if you had money . . . not ever!

And the beaver . . . they didn't exactly belong to anyone . . . in particular . . . even Brant admitted that!

Webb wondered why he was thinking this way. It was now more than two weeks, almost three, since that trip to Needles, when the fur buyer had made contact with

him, and since the burning of the tule island the next
morning.

Maybe it was Brant's visit yesterday that had kicked him
off into the mixed-up thoughts. There had been talk about
beaver, the night before. A lot of talk, Webb remembered!

He had never seen the game ranger so enthusiastic about
anything. There had been many good reasons for that.
The trapping had been good; Brant had reported on the
pelts that had already been sold. The price they brought
had surprised everybody—an average of forty-nine dollars
each! The news that had flabbergasted everybody, especially Tom, was that the light-colored, the silver pelts had
sold best!

It wasn't any wonder that the man in Needles had
offered Webb double what the game departments of
Arizona and California were paying him for catching the
beaver, and that he'd been willing to jump the price to
fifteen dollars a pelt!

It made Webb realize that he and Tom were getting
little enough for their work. That turned his thoughts to
his partner, and he listened for the old man's snoring.
There wasn't a sound coming from the bunk on the other
side of the tent.

Webb threw the covers aside, pulled on his clothes and
stepped out of the tent onto the deck of the pontoon float.

"Mornin'!" The brief greeting came from the early gloom
of the river bank.

Tom grinned ruefully, his good eye sparkling with feeling.

"Those tule burners won't catch me in bed again. Besides, I'm fixin' traps today. There's a dozen or more need-
in' new springs and chains before we move up the river
to the beach."

"Gosh!" exclaimed Webb. "It's hard to realize that fire happened over three weeks ago."

"Been too busy to think," crabbed Tom. "You've been bringing in so many pigs, it's all I can do to keep my knives sharp."

"How many have we cured?" asked Webb. He was a little surprised to realize that he had forgotten the exact number.

" 'Bout three hundred. We've got about fifteen hundred dollars comin' to split between us."

Webb fell silent then, busying himself with getting his boat ready for the day's work. But his mind turned over the conversation again. His share would be seven hundred and fifty dollars. This would have sounded like the U. S. Mint a month ago, but now it didn't. The same amount of furs sold to the contraband fur buyers would have brought him three thousand at their first offer, four thousand five hundred at the second offer. The states, Arizona and California, were getting over fifteen thousand dollars for the pelts, as against his seven hundred and fifty. Webb couldn't help but feel it wasn't quite fair. The more he thought about it, the more unreasonable it seemed.

"I'm staying out all day today," he announced to Tom. "I'm pulling all the traps this morning, and I'm going to build a goose hunting blind this afternoon, and put out some decoys."

"Atta boy!" said Tom, with rare mellowness, "We'll celebrate Thanksgiving with roast honker—if you can hit 'em!"

"Just get the pan ready." Webb nodded, falling in with Tom's unaccustomed mood of fun.

"Yeah? Duck huntin' calls for a sharp shootin' eye!" jeered Tom.

"Just be ready, that's all." Webb was noncommittal

about his shooting ability, although he knew what he could do with either the rifle or his repeating shotgun.

Tom winked his one good eye knowingly and went back to his traps.

Webb trimmed his boat for the day's work. He called Champ, who was just finishing up the breakfast scraps, and cast off. He was waiting for the boat to drift free when Tom again stepped into sight on the high bank and looked down.

"I was just thinkin', Webb. Luck's breakin' your way. Brant's bringin' the judge out tonight. You oughta set your sights."

Webb frowned and was about to ask for an explanation of the odd remark when Tom turned back and disappeared. The trapper's enigmatic words gave Webb something to think about while he pulled the beaver sets. He was still mulling them over toward midafternoon when he had finished gathering the traps and had run to the upper end of the Slough. There he soon found the low island that he and Brant had seen on the survey, the one he had marked in his mind as an ideal place for a goose and duck hunting blind.

Webb began to feel a rising anticipation of the goose hunting to come in the next few days. The feeling was high in him when he beached the boat on the island.

"Come here, Champ!" he called. The dog came and Webb knelt by him, fondling the rough coat for a moment. "Here's where you'll get a real workout, ol' boy."

He sent the retriever scampering ahead, and walked to the center of the long silt bar the Colorado River had cast up near midchannel. A conglomerate pile of driftwood marked the highest part of the island, the center. Level sand tapered to a point upstream. It was sparsely feathered

110

with newly-sprouting tules. Some of the higher ground had ragged growths of Bermuda grass. The lower half of the island stretched out flat, almost at river level, and it was marked with potholes of water.

"Ready-made," said Webb, surveying the bar from his stand among the piled driftwood. He rolled Champ over in a feeling of delight at what was to come. The Labrador growled in mock anger and they locked in simulated combat, rolling over and over in the sand. Champ's steel-muscled jaws snapped together a fraction of an inch from Webb's throat again and again as they tussled. Finally, Webb, exhausted, called a halt to the romp. He still had work to do.

He spent a half-hour constructing a shooting blind in the driftwood, excavating a pit and screening it with willows and tules. When it was finished to his satisfaction, he set out the decoys. Then he called to Champ and put the Labrador through several obedience and retrieving drills, working him out of the blind.

"You're perfect, a real champion," praised Webb, petting his dog. Suddenly, and impulsively, he dropped alongside the golden retriever and hugged him close. Champ squirmed happily, thinking the romp was to begin again. Webb quieted him with a calming hand.

"Dog, you're about all I've got, or ever will have, I guess."

Champ bowed his powerful neck to lay his head on the encircling arms.

The Colorado whispered against the bank, looking like molten metal to Webb, as it reflected the setting sun. He stared into space as he fondled the retriever and thought about the beaver trapping and the offer made by the contrabanders and Brant—but, most of all he thought

111

about himself, wondering what the future had for him.

His reverie was interrupted by the distant yelp-yelp-yelping of lonesome geese winging down the river. They were in sight, stitched evenly across the darkening sky.

Webb shivered slightly, partly from the cold wind and partly from the excitement of the approaching geese. The feeling of lonesomeness crept upon him and he pulled the big dog close. The animal's body heat was soon warming him, inside and out.

The leader of the geese saw the decoys and circled warily, then set his wings and led the flock to a landing at the upper end of the island.

Webb watched for a moment, then, with Champ at heel, he slipped out of the back of the blind. Together they went to the boat.

Brant's boat was tied to the pontoons of the barge when Webb coasted up, just after dark. A campfire, out of sight behind the high bank, threw a flickering light on the leafless cottonwoods. Then the figure of a man appeared silhouetted against the trees. The outlines were unfamiliar and Webb tensed. But just then the compact body of the ranger stepped into sight, and Webb knew then that the other was Judge Schaulkler!

"Hi, Kid!" called Brant, leaping nimbly down the bank and onto the pontoons. "Toss me that tie-rope."

Suddenly a feeling of uneasiness swept over Webb. This would be the first time he had seen the judge since he had walked out of the jurist's office with Brant. . . . He felt the game ranger's balled fist come up and jar him gently in the jaw, causing him to raise his head so that he had to look into Brant's eyes.

"The judge is on your side, Kid," the cocky little man

said in an undertone. "Don't forget it. He's out here for two reasons: to go goose hunting with you and to see how you're getting along—and, Buster, I'm going to tell him 'Fine!' Don't cross me up!"

Webb shook his head. "I won't." And he knew he meant it. Those few hours alone at the goose blind with Champ had cleared his thinking. He had almost decided to make a deal with the contraband fur buyers if he ever had another chance. He knew that now.

"I talked like a Dutch uncle for your parole, didn't I?"

Webb had to agree to that. He nodded.

"Okay then, forget he's a judge of superior court. You'll find out he's a real sport, a man who likes duck and goose hunting just as well as you do."

Webb followed Brant up the river bank to where Judge Schaulkler waited. The dignified and bespectacled jurist reached out a warm and surprisingly strong hand.

"How are you, Webb? And your Labrador?"

"Pretty good," admitted Webb shyly. "Champ, he's great, and ready to work."

The judge put an arm across his shoulders. "Brant's reports about you have been very good. You're doing fine. And Mr. Jesson tells me you're making a real beaver trapper."

Webb twisted uncomfortably. Seldom had anyone, man or woman, ever shown affection for him.

"Excuse me, Judge." The game ranger grinned at his own boldness. "You're in our court now and Tom's got supper ready, and we've got goose hunting business to talk over."

As they walked to the fire, where Tom squatted with his ovens, the ranger turned to Webb again.

"Any honkers hanging around?"

Judge Schaulkler, slipping into the easy informality of a hunting camp, spoke before Webb could reply to Brant.

"I forgot to tell you—coming down I picked up a weather report on my car radio. A blizzard has covered northern Utah, Idaho and Montana during the last two days. That should send geese down."

"It has," said Webb. "A new flock—about thirty-five birds —came down the river this afternoon. We'll have a good hunt tomorrow."

"Grub's ready," announced Tom tersely, clanging a Dutch oven lid as he inspected the biscuits. "Let's eat."

Webb listened quietly as the others talked while they ate. After the meal, the judge and Brant both lit their pipes. The latter leaned back against his still-tied bedroll.

Webb caught a smile twisting at the corners of the mobile mouth of the game ranger.

"This is something I've been saving for the right time, and I guess this is it," drawled the officer teasingly, sliding a look out of the corner of his eyes at Webb. "As you all know, that first shipment of beaver topped the market at the Seattle Fur Exchange." He puffed a moment, then looked at Tom. Here, Webb realized, was the news Brant had savored. "And," the officer continued, "those light-colored beaver are demanding better prices."

"I'll be danged!" the old trapper muttered, scowling as he scratched his balding head.

"The silver beaver blankets were running sixty dollars a pelt. That second lot averaged out fifty-one fifty, because of all those light beaver you've been catching!"

"They musta had a Forty-second street dude doin' the gradin'," snorted Tom, spitting into the fire, which sputtered and smoked protestingly.

"Excuse me for being a dude," interrupted the judge with a smile, "but what is a beaver blanket?"

"A size of beaver pelt," replied Brant. Then, turning to Webb, he added, "Just how does it go? I don't remember."

Webb looked at the warm light in his friend's crinkly brown eyes and he knew the game ranger had pled ignorance on purpose, to get him into the conversation.

"Can you tell me?" asked the judge, leaning forward curiously.

Webb picked up a stick. He felt a little foolish trying to tell the judge anything, but he smoothed off the ground in front of the fire and drew a circle.

"A beaver pelt is stretched round. The number of inches from the nose to the tail and from side to side gives you the size."

He looked at Brant with embarrassment as he pulled a notebook out of his pocket, one that he had bought after being with the ranger on the beaver survey. It was just like the officer's.

"I've got to look," he explained. "A blanket is sixty-five inches or over and is usually marked X-X-L, meaning extra-extra-large, I guess. The next size, extra-large, or X-L, has to measure fifty-nine inches or over. The large measure is fifty inches, a medium forty-five or on up to fifty, and a small is forty inches and up. Anything under forty inches is called a cub or kit."

Brant beamed proudly. "Webb knows his beaver," he declared with satisfaction.

"He does, he does." The judge nodded thoughtfully. Then he chuckled, "Sounds as though a California publicity writer had something to do with naming the different grades—*extra-extra-large!*"

Everyone laughed at the witticism and Webb began to feel more relaxed. The judge seemed like a regular sort of a guy. He was acting just like any man would in camp.

"Tom, this will get you," warned Brant. "Those lighter beaver—the fur buyers saw something special about them, and they called them 'silver beaver,' too!"

The old man rubbed his thinning hair, a puzzled expression on his face. He poked at the fire vigorously before growling, "They're freak beaver, Judge. They ain't—or weren't—worth a puffa smoke in a whirlwind 'longside a good dark skin . . . an' they wouldn't be now if them buyers had any sense!"

Brant chuckled. "The best of Stetson's hats are made from beaver. You know that, don't you?"

Tom nodded. "Sure I know it—their seven X is called a 'Silver Beaver.' I paid fifty dollars for one once, when I was a young stallion, with more cash than sense."

They all laughed at the trapper's comment.

"The garment makers took a fancy to the light beaver," Brant went on. "They figure they can make a new style

116

coat called 'The Platinum' that will create a demand for itself and sell for hundreds of dollars, or maybe a couple of thousand! They want the natural silver beaver for these coats—and it seems this part of the Colorado River is the only place where beaver of such a shade have been trapped." Brant studied the fire. "If the idea catches on, we might see those silver beaver go to seventy and maybe eighty bucks a blanket."

The older trapper poked at the fire, his lips working as if he were about to speak. Suddenly he got up.

"G'night, I'm going to bed. I'm just an *old* beaver skinner!"

The judge scrambled to his feet. "Don't take it so hard, Tom. I'm just an old judge. It's a young man's world . . . for fellows like Webb here."

The two left Webb and the game ranger alone by the fire. Brant untied and unrolled his bed.

"How about getting yours, Kid, and sleeping up here with me?"

That was to Webb's liking. He liked sleeping in the open, under the sky, and he liked especially being asked by the game ranger . . . and to have Champ curled up on his bed tarp alongside him.

12

THE JUDGE DISCOVERS WEBB'S
LABRADOR IS REGISTERED

Champ woke Webb by getting up to change positions.
The pale, low-hung moon was a formless blob in the
cloudy sky. Webb raised his head, listening: there was the
steady lapping of the river at the bank and the sides of
the pontoon barge, and the wind strumming in the leafless
branches overhead.

He could feel it in his bones . . . this would be a day
of days to hunt geese! And it was time to get up! He
leaped to his feet, shaking out his rolled-up Levis.

"Yowie!" yelled Brant as he woke and stuck his head
from under his bed tarp. "Wow! It's cold!"

"We'll eat in the tent this morning," shouted Webb,
clumping down the bank and storming into the shelter
on the float. His noisy entrance woke the judge and Tom,
and he busied himself building a fire in the flat-topped
sheet iron stove while they directed kidding insults his
way.

The stimulating cold made Webb forget his self-imposed

reserve in front of Judge Schaulkler, and he soon presented Tom and the judge with a cup of steaming coffee to fondle and sip as they dressed.

Tom hurried them through breakfast.

"You three git on, I'll do the dishes. But listen, Webb," he reminded the boy, "I'm sharpenin' up my store teeth for roast goose!"

When Brant called, "All clear," Webb started the motor. It was still dark. Champ was excited, and the boy had some difficulty keeping the dog quiet.

"He must know we're going hunting," said the judge around his pipestem, the bowl glowing in the dark.

"Sure he does," agreed Brant. "He feels just like I do, probably. What do you think, Webb? Is it going to be good?"

"Perfect. It's just right: cold, windy. They'll be flying this morning."

Almost an hour later, just as the eastern sky was beginning to pale, Webb beached the boat on the island near the driftwood.

"The blind is right in the middle," he directed the others. "You two get in, and I'll take the boat back to the lower end and hide it."

Fifteen minutes later, Webb, with the dog at his heels, slid into the blind. The judge and Brant were already settling down, arranging their shotguns and shells on the edge.

Webb stood up a moment, taking one last look around in the rapidly strengthening light. It was a better goose shooting setup than he had realized. The long, scimitar-shaped island followed the direction of the river. The blunt upper end was close to water level, and the tapering lower end was pocked with waterholes. Tules were beginning to grow there. He looked again to make sure. Yes, the boat was hidden.

A scattering of duck decoys floated on the potholes where he had dropped them.

Then he looked to the goose decoys at the upper end of the island. Something dissatisfied him there, and commanding Champ to drop, he ran to the set. He picked up one or two decoys as he hurried through to the head of the group and reset these. As he came back, he turned each one so its head was to the wind.

He raced back to the blind, ordered Champ into the pit and then jumped down himself.

Judge Schaulkler was beaming with enthusiasm.

"This is wonderful, Webb, absolutely wonderful. The best blind I've ever been in, and I've sat in quite a few!"

"It's a natural setup," the boy admitted, turning the screen of willows at a partial angle, to cover the pit, yet set so it could be pushed aside in an instant. "It was ready-made."

"Maybe so, but it takes a goose hunter to see that." The judge paused a moment, then continued, "Now, Webb, you're in charge here, so tell me what to do and when to do it."

The slightly uncomfortable feeling of the evening before came back to Webb. Here he was, on probation from the judge's court, yet the judge was asking him what to do. But mixed with that feeling was an inside glow, a sort of building excitement and warmth for the man. The judge was a real, honest-to-gosh sport!

Webb managed a sidewise grin.

"Well, if you're asking for it: just don't move. Don't move, even to look at them when they fly around in back of us. If they'll decoy, they'll come down into the set.

That's in front of us. So, don't move a finger until you get up to shoot."

"I'll wait for your word," approved the judge, cupping his hands around his glowing pipe bowl to warm them.

Webb shoved his own red, chapped hands into the torn sleeves of his leather jacket. He and Brant stood up, looking this way and that over the horizon. Day was coming fast now, a wintry day, with low-flying clouds. It was quiet, except for the washing of the river on the nearby shore.

"I hear 'em!" Brant said finally. He became suddenly tense beside Webb.

"Yeah, there's a flight coming downriver," Webb confirmed. "See them, just over that flat-topped mesa?"

The two lowered themselves behind the screening blind. Webb glanced at the judge, who was waiting philosophically, but with eyes shining from inner excitement. He reached over and gripped Webb on the forearm.

The "cad-dia-lac-ing" of the geese became increasingly louder, then the pit resounded with the metallic clicking of shells and readied actions.

"Quiet!" warned Webb, putting a hand down on Champ. The dog quivered, then remained still.

Webb put his goose call to his mouth; a yelping noise came from it. The even-flying wedge of geese swerved, swinging almost imperceptibly toward the decoys. The leaders called. Webb did not reply. The flock circled to the left, behind the hunters, and appeared again on the right, a quarter of a mile away.

Webb called again, giving a low "Eeee-yonk," as the flock, on whistling wings, passed closer this time.

The circle the geese made was smaller now, and the third time around they passed directly overhead, flying into the wind. Webb talked to them in low conversational tones on his caller.

The leader glided downwind, losing altitude, the flock tumbling down behind him.

Although he did not turn his head to follow the flight, Webb knew the geese were turning into the wind, and would pass directly over the blind with set wings, braking for a landing. As the big birds slowed to a stalling speed over the set, they flapped their wings and let their feet down.

"Now!" said Webb, his voice crackling with excitement as he picked up his shotgun. But he held his fire.

The lead goose collapsed to the salute of the judge's double-barrel. The second goose in line tucked up his trailing feet and scaffled. The rest, too, beat their wings for altitude and to gain flying speed.

Webb raised his shotgun, smoothly injecting a shell. The last goose in line was flying low and fast. Webb saw him over the sights, and then, swinging to lead the target, he squeezed the trigger. The gun roared and nudged him.

The goose fell, pinwheeling to the water on half-stretched wings. The others were out of gun range.

"Go!" commanded Webb, waving Champ forward. The Labrador raced into the shallow water and came back, stepping high and proudly, carrying the goose Webb had dropped. Then Webb sent him out to recover the judge's goose, which was lying among the decoys.

"I never got a shot," Brant admitted with a rueful laugh. "I was just about to pull the trigger on that leader when you dropped him out from under my sight, Judge!"

"Oh, I'm sorry, Brant!"

"Think nothing of it, my friend," said the ranger, straight-

Webb called again, giving a low "Eeee-yonk," as the flock, on whistling wings, passed closer this time

ening his hat to shield his eyes as he looked upriver. "Down! Down!"

Webb and the judge dropped without looking around. "Three, coming right down the river!"

The hunters couldn't see the geese. They didn't dare raise their heads to look. It wasn't until the birds had passed the blind, flying downwind, that Webb did see them. He called to the trio, flying in line, and they turned.

The geese circled warily, wide and high, gradually getting closer. Webb talked to them on the caller, but the leader swerved away, turning out of his fourth circle.

Webb grabbed his old felt hat and sailed it out over the decoys.

Quickly he called again. The notes sounded plaintive and lonesome.

The leader of the trio, scudding before the wind, looked back and saw the fluttering hat, then, apparently mistaking it for another goose, just as Webb had hoped, he stretched his wings and was settling again. He whirled in a descending turn and came into the wind. The three birds cupped their wings.

The judge, unable to contain himself, whispered, "Decoyed! Wonderfully skillful, Webb!"

The hunters waited until the geese let their feet down, then Webb gave the word.

"Shoot first," the judge urged Brant. The judge's gun honored the ranger's blast. Two geese collapsed in mid-flight. One dropped like a stone. The other caught itself and turned downwind, flying just above the water, to gain a hundred yards before it splashed in mid-channel.

"Go!" yelled Webb. Champ leaped up and out, racing for the dead bird in the blinds. Webb whistled sharply, once. The retriever skidded to a stop in mid-stride, looked back. Webb waved him to the river, in the direction of the floating goose. The dog faltered, unable to see the bird. Webb whistled again, and redirected the big Labrador.

Then Champ saw the floating bird and leaped far out into the cold water.

"Webb, you've got a field trial dog there!" exclaimed the judge, as he watched Champ perform on the complicated retrieve. "He's a marvel. Where did you get him?"

Webb hesitated, at loss for words. He had never been quite comfortable when called upon to explain his possession of the Labrador, especially in front of Brant.

Champ had reached the goose, picked it up and turned upstream. The strong current had already carried the retriever below the tail of the island. But Champ, swimming powerfully, holding the goose high, appeared to be making good headway.

"He certainly shows his blood," the judge said admiringly.

"What do you mean?" asked Webb. "He's just a yellow dog that likes to hunt, as far as I'm concerned," he confessed with a proud grin.

"I will wager he's of good Labrador stock," said the judge stubbornly, "the purest strain of dogs ever developed."

The three hunters stood on the rise, watching the retriever battle the current. Webb called encouragement. Champ shifted the goose until it trailed over his shoulder and drove harder, gaining speed.

"An interesting strain," continued the judge, nodding wisely. "The Labrador is really out of Newfoundland stock. Back in the early 1800's, they were used as ship dogs—before rocket guns were invented—for carrying a line from ship to shore. The sailors would attach a line to a dog and drop him overboard. The animal was trained to swim to shore, through pounding surf. The people on land would then pull the line and bring a ship's hawser to shore."

Webb was listening closely. This was something new, and he liked the intense feeling it gave him for his dog.

Finally Champ reached them, dripping with water but holding the goose high for his beaming young master to take.

"May I pet him, Webb?" asked the judge.

"Why, sure!"

The judge fondled the dog. "Some owners don't like to have strangers show affection for their dogs, and they have a point if theirs are working dogs."

Webb's heart gave a thump of apprehension as the judge lifted Champ's ears and looked inside.

"H'mm! Just as I thought." The judge nodded, tilting his head to see through his bifocals. "He's a registered dog!"

The jurist put his finger on the dots inside one ear. "This is a symbol, a code! Your dog has a pedigree, Webb. We can trace his ancestry and his ownership through these marks."

Webb's teeth shut on sudden, rising anger. He drew back, pulling Champ with him.

"He's mine! I found him . . . sure, but he would have died in the Slough. I don't want . . ."

The judge's brows were raised in surprise. Brant stepped forward, raising a hand to stop the boy's torrent of words.

"Relax, Kid." The ranger spoke softly. "You're not going to lose that dog. Of course you have a right to him. The judge isn't going to take him; he didn't have that in mind at all."

"Why, I should say not, Webb," said the judge quickly, chagrin on his face as he saw how he had disturbed the boy. "Please don't think I'd want you to lose Champ. I was only thinking that if he's pedigreed and registered, he would be eligible for field trials."

"Can't you just forget it, Judge?" Webb asked unhappily. "I don't care whether Champ's a pedigreed dog or not. It doesn't make a bit of difference to me. I just couldn't take it if I had to give him up."

Judge Schaulkler tilted his head and rubbed his chin, which was beginning to show a grizzled whiskering.

"Of course, legally, the ownership of the dog apparently rests with someone else, Webb. You found him, true. But," the jurist paused a moment, then broke into a wide smile, "considering this as your lawyer—and I would defend your claim, if necessary—you could establish a just claim on Champ for board, care and training. The evidence would undoubtedly be strong enough to establish legal ownership. At least, we could take it to court on that basis."

Brant laughed. "And, you bet we would, Kid!" he asserted.

Webb searched their faces. He sensed that he could be sure they were telling him the truth, yet he held back. The possibility of losing Champ had hit him hard. It left him feeling sickish.

"Okay, I understand," he mumbled, then fell silent. The fun had gone out of the hunt for him, though, and he couldn't help showing it.

Another flock of geese came in to interrupt the conversation. Both the judge and the ranger bagged a goose out of the flight. Webb didn't shoot.

"That fills us," said Brant, unloading his shotgun. "Now,

127

let's start back to camp. I want to get the pelts ready—
the ones you and Tom have finished curing. I'll come back
in a day or two and help you move to Willow Beach. In
the meantime, Webb, you can hunt."

Webb nodded, but with little expression. He was still
worried about what Judge Schaulkler might do about
tracing Champ's ancestry.

As Webb and Brant were loading the boat, it happened
that the judge was down at the water's edge and they
were alone in the pit. The ranger reached out, placed both
hands on Webb's shoulders and turned him around.

"Look, Kid, don't worry about the dog. He's yours now,
and no one will take him away from you. I'll guarantee
that and make it stick."

Webb shook his head apprehensively. "But there's the
legal angle . . ."

"Didn't you hear the judge? Now, don't worry; you're
among friends." The officer stopped suddenly and looked
beyond Webb toward the distant California shore of the
river. "Some hunters over there; I just caught the sun
glinting off a gun barrel or a pair of field glasses."

"I guess they didn't get any shooting," said Webb. "At
least I didn't hear any shots."

Brant threw an arm around the boy's shoulders. "Well,
we sure did. Webb, you're a good guide, a top guide."

"I'm in accord with that," said the judge as he walked
up to the blind.

On the way back to the camp, the judge was lavish in
his expressions of appreciation for the good hunt.

"You should do something with your skill, Webb. You
seem to have a natural ability for all this outdoor living,"
he said seriously. "For example, it takes a great deal of
patience and wisdom to teach a dog to do the things

Champ did for us." He hesitated, then went on, "By the way, what are you hoping to do when you . . . for a life work?"

The change of subject was welcomed by Webb; anything to get the judge's mind off tracing Champ's registration.

"I don't really know . . . trap, I guess. Maybe guide hunters and fishermen."

The judge pursed his lips, then said lightly, "That's . . . fine . . . for a while, but you'd want to aim higher, wouldn't you, for a full-time career?"

Webb was about to retort with "What's wrong with that?" but he thought better of it. He didn't want to antagonize the judge by deliberate rudeness.

"I haven't got the money to go on to school. If I could, I might like working for the game department, doing something like Brant's doing."

"Very good, I'd say." The judge nodded approvingly. "You would no doubt enjoy out-of-door work most, and you'd probably be a success. There are some very good positions to be had in the field of wildlife management, but all of them take a higher education."

"And I can't get that, so there's no chance," Webb said flatly. For the first time in his life he felt a peculiar stirring. Something in what the judge had said roused strange longings in the boy. He looked at the judge, who was obviously thinking earnestly as he busied himself with his pipe. He tamped it full of tobacco, then knocked it out without even lighting it! At last he spoke to Brant.

"My friend, I've got a bit of business to talk over with you on the way home tomorrow; just remind me." Then he turned back to the boy. "Never give up hope, Webb. Things do not remain the same. They get worse or they get better, and for you, I believe they will get better. Just keep on doing the good job you are doing."

The rest of the way was traveled in almost complete silence, except for the roar of the boat's motor. Darkness was settling over the Slough, and Webb's mind went back to the day before, when Tom had said, "Set your sights while luck's breakin' your way."

13.

WEBB CROSSES THE FUR RACKETEERS

Judge Schaulkler and Brant had left the camp for town just before noon. Since then, Webb had been busying himself with sorting traps, gathering up tools and readying the gear for the move to Willow Beach, which was to be made in a few days.

It was almost midafternoon when his mental reviewing of the incidents of the hunt the day before were interrupted by the uneven puttering of a poorly-running outboard. Soon the boat came into sight. A lone man sat in the stern.

The stranger was heading for the barge. As he approached, Webb recognized him as an amateur boatman, for instead of swinging below and coming up against the current and alongside the pontoons, the man drove straight in. Webb had to lean down and hold back the sharp prow to keep it from ramming the thin plywood hull of the float.

"Thanks for catching it," the stranger said, clambering

131

awkwardly over the boat seats and onto the barge, with Webb's help. The man put out his hand in friendly greeting. It was soft and cold.

"Usually have a fellow run it for me—knows how to handle boats. Not my line." The man smiled expansively, showing a line of strong, polished teeth. "I'm Richard Savote, S-A-V-O-T-E. Who's in charge here? You?" the man demanded, rather than asked, speaking quickly and clipping his words.

"No one in particular," replied Webb, undecided whether or not he liked the breezy stranger. "There're just Tom Jesson and me. We're trappers."

"Oh?" questioned the stranger, raising his heavy eyebrows. Webb noticed the piercing light gray eyes, which were too pale for the rest of the man's coloring. They registered everything in swift, shooting glances.

"You were hunting geese yesterday morning, weren't you?"

"Yes," admitted Webb, then wondered why he had replied so readily.

The stranger's smile was disarmingly warm as he said, "We were too, across the river. Never got a shot." The man pulled a zipper on his down-filled jacket, revealing a shirt pocket stuffed with cigars. He took out three, offered one to Webb.

"Thanks, I don't smoke."

"Never turn down a thing, Kid, not when it's for free! Give 'em to your partner."

Tom, a few yards away, had never stopped whetting his skinning knives, even when the stranger walked up on the bank above the float. Webb saw the old trapper look up at the stranger, the one eye glistening as sharp as a diamond point as it surveyed the stranger.

"Watched your retriever work through these field glasses," mouthed Savote around his cigar as he unbuttoned his shirt and took out an expensive pair of binoculars which were hung on a short strap around his neck. "You've got a good dog there." He paused to bite off the end of the cigar and lighted it. "That's what I came over for; I'd like to hire you and the dog, and rent your blind for tomorrow. How about it?"

"Well, I don't know," Webb began. "We're moving camp in a couple of days and . . ."

Savote waved his hand impatiently. "Figure it out. I'll pay—pay your partner for doubling up, and pay you for guiding. A deal?"

Tom got up then. "It's jake with me, Webb," he said. "The work's mostly caught up."

The prospect of some ready cash was interesting, even if he didn't care too much for this dude sportsman, Webb decided.

"Okay, I'll go."

Savote rubbed his hands together expressively.

"Ah, fine!" He pulled a packet of bills out of his pocket. It was then that Webb noticed the gold clip—the design looked familiar, he thought. Where had he seen one like it before? He watched as Savote peeled back some twenties and then stripped out a ten, which he gave to Tom.

"Thanks." Savote grinned at the expressionless old man. "You're a right guy!"

Tom accepted the money and comment without expression, except for a nod as he lit one of the cigars the man had given him.

"Now," continued Savote, turning to Webb, "meet us at your blind just before daylight. There'll be two of us.

Don't bring any food or shells; we'll have all we need. What gauge do you have?"

"Twelve, and I like double-ought for geese."

"Check!"

The man took out his packet of bills again, peeled off another ten, which he gave to Webb. Then he unfolded the packet, showing ones and fives on the inside. He took out one of the fives and passed it to Tom.

"You've got to get a fair shake out of this deal, ol' timer, and this will cinch it."

There was finality in Savote's voice. His manner indicated he was used to being obeyed. He talked like an autoloading rifle, thought Webb, one that could be shot in bursts of words.

The man climbed down the bank and into his boat. He drifted far downstream before he could get the motor started. Webb watched him until he disappeared.

On the way to the blind the following morning, the chill of the pre-dawn gloom pressed Webb. He felt a twinge of misgiving. Now he remembered the gold clip on the packet; it was identical to the one the sharpie in Needles had on his roll. He suppressed a chilly feeling of trouble, reminding himself that anyone could happen to buy a similar bill clip.

He reached out to pet Champ, and felt better right away. Somehow the presence of the dog always helped him over bad feelings and bad times. He never felt quite alone when he could put out his hand and touch the rough coat.

"You're a real partner in a tight," he murmured.

Champ moved his tail, which hung over the edge of the deck. Otherwise he gave no sign that he had heard his master speak. Webb had to laugh to himself, inside. Champ was all business, now that he knew they were going hunting again.

When Webb's boat reached the island, the two hunters had not yet arrived, so he hid his craft in the tules and went to the blind, where he made some improvements. Then he built a tiny fire to warm his hands while he waited. The storm that had been building in the northern states was moving into Arizona. He looked up; the sky promised bad weather—which meant good hunting!

It was ten minutes before he heard the popping of an outboard, and he knew the hunters would soon be there. As he listened, he detected the sound of another motor. But only one boat came out of the morning fog that was drifting off the warmer river into the cold morning air. The sound of the other boat slanted away as it went to the far California shore.

Webb met the boat at the water's edge. Savote sat in front. At the tiller of the motor was the man who had come to the motel and offered Webb the money, to steal the beaver pelts!

Now the boy knew his feeling about the clips had been right in the first place!

"Morning, Webb." Savote grinned, handing out a leather-cased shotgun. Then, seeing the consternation on the boy's face, he added, "Relax, Buster, we came to hunt geese; that's on the level. Maybe talk a little business later, but not now. Let's get set up." He turned to the man in the boat. "This is Milt Krakow, Webb. I don't think you caught his name the other time you met; at least he hasn't heard from you," Savote added over-casually.

Webb didn't seem to be able to cope with the confusion in his mind, so he said nothing. He automatically helped

135

with the unloading of the boat, and then pulled it off so it floated downstream to the tules. By that time he knew where he stood. Savote had hired him to serve as guide and for the rental of the blind and use of the retriever, but any fur deals would be out.

"Here, Webb, this'll warm you up." Savote offered him a cup of steaming coffee that he had poured out of a thermos jug. "It's going to be a cold day."

Webb took the hot cup in his cold-chapped hands. It felt good and tasted better. He spoke a reserved, "Thanks."

"You've got sore hands, Webb. Saw that yesterday, and brought this along for you." He held out an oversized mitten for a left hand. "Slip it on. Come on, put it on."

Webb shoved his left hand into the huge mitten and was surprised to feel it warm on the inside, the heat seeming to be on the back.

"You slip your right hand into the pocket on the back. Use it like a muff."

Savote took Webb's cup and guided the boy's right hand into place. Inside was a metal object that fit into Webb's palm and glowed with inner heat. He pulled it out to look at it.

"Handwarmer." Savote grinned, lighting up a fresh cigar. "New gadget for sportsmen. I had the mittens made up special. Nice, eh? That one's yours."

Webb had to agree; it was nice. For the first time he realized how cold his hands had been. Funny how you can sort of get used to discomfort, he thought, but he shivered slightly as the wind suddenly strengthened and blew across the island. His old worn leather jacket didn't turn the sharp knives of the wind.

The man called Milt saw the involuntary shudder, and he stripped off his canvas hunting coat. As Webb watched, fascinated, the man pulled one of several zippers and unfastened a down jacket from the inside. The down lining was really a second garment. This he forced onto Webb.

"Even if we can't do business, there's no need for you to freeze—not when we've got all these clothes along." He indicated his own warm woolen shirt under the canvas jacket.

Webb had never worn a down-filled jacket before. Its lightness and warmth astounded him, and he couldn't help feeling gratitude for the generosity of the men.

He watched as they took their shotguns out of the cases and put them together.

Savote handed his to Webb.

"New Magnum, special made." As Webb took it and swung it to his shoulder, hefting it and getting its feel, Savote added, meaningfully, "Takes money for these things. Cost me five hundred."

As the morning went on, several flocks of geese came down the river, riding the hard wind. Some flapped right on by, but Webb managed to bring two down within range of the guns. It was well into the afternoon before Savote and Milt each had one goose, however.

Still, the day had been pleasant enough, even though it was turning colder and windier. Savote had opened a hamper of warm food, there was another thermos of coffee. They even had food for Champ, which Savote jovially insisted on feeding him. Webb had almost relaxed under the generosity and camaraderie extended him by the two. His long training in wariness under his uncle's teaching wouldn't let him completely overcome a suspicion, a little doubt, however. It was too planned, even if it was pleasant —and comfortable.

Webb looked to the west.

"It's going to get dark early, with this cloudy sky. When do you think you want to quit?"

"Pretty soon," replied Savote, sipping on hot coffee. I'd like to talk . . ."

"Heads up!" interrupted Milt. "String of geese coming!"

"Talk 'em down," said Savote, setting his coffee cup on the ground. "If you do, Webb, there'll be money in it for you."

The honkers were traveling high, taking advantage of the wind bringing the storm from the north. Webb waited until the leader swerved slightly, indicating he had sighted the decoys. The boy called, loudly this time, to carry above the stronger wind. The flock turned and came down in a steady glide that terminated over the set, and Webb changed from a noisy calling to a conversational gaggling.

The burst of shotgun fire dropped three geese; one was dead as it hit the ground. The two cripples managed to drop into the river. A blast from Savote's Magnum killed one, but the other swam out of range.

"Let's see you work the dog on that one," urged Savote.

Champ went after the cripple first, at Webb's direction, then he leaped into the water again, to swim after the dead goose that had already floated a long distance.

Savote shook his head in admiration.

"Flawless. A flawless retriever. You ought to work him in field trials." He turned, looking at Webb calculatingly. "How'd you like to take him up to Canada and put him up against some real competition?"

"My money would be on Champ," Milt said unhesitatingly. "You could win yourself a wad of folding money."

Webb's mind was stimulated by the man's words. Yesterday it had been the judge who had excited his imagination, but this was easy money, and it looked good to the boy . . . nothing crooked about it, either.

Champ trotted toward them and sat down on the edge of the pit, waiting for Webb to take the last goose.

"Will he hold it?" asked Savote, reaching into a duffel bag. "I want a picture of that!" He took several pictures, then he turned.

"Webb, how would you like to see Champ sitting like that with a bank of gold and silver trophy cups in front of him? Be great, wouldn't it?"

Webb started to speak, but Savote interrupted. "Sure, I know—you haven't got the money." He paused significantly. "But you could have. You've shipped a couple or three hundred already. They'd never have missed twenty, thirty, even fifty. And at fifteen bucks apiece, you would have had all your pockets full of dough by now."

Savote leaned forward, stopping Webb's comment with a big, white hand upraised.

"They've given you a song and dance about beaver management being the property of the people. That kills me! Let me ask you, Webb: who's taking the big cut out of your deal?"

Webb stammered his answer, then wished he had kept still. "The state of Arizona, and California. They're getting most of . . ."

"Right! And I'll lay you ten to one somebody's creaming off the top."

"I don't see how . . ." replied Webb, beginning to feel a little indignant at the constant interruption.

"Get smart, boy. Wherever there's money, there are ways," the man went on. "There's money in beaver and you're not getting your share of the cut."

Webb tried to organize his whirling thoughts. One

thing came out: here was opportunity again—a chance to make some money.

Savote looked at him sharply and pressed his advantage, his words beating on Webb's ears with staccato rapidity.

"Milt, fill Webb's cup. Listen, boy, I like you and I'll cut you a deal. This beaver market is big. It's red-hot, and I've got it rigged. I've got a buyer in Albuquerque to legalize Arizona pelts. I've got another in Cheyenne putting plums on Colorado, Montana and Idaho beaver. I've got a fix in L.A. My stuff doesn't go through the regular market in Seattle. It goes straight to town—that's New York —and right into coats."

Savote tapped Webb on the chest, poking him with a big finger. As he did so, a diamond on the same hand caught the light and shattered it into fiery brilliance.

"But the biggest thing that's happened this season," Savote went on, eyebrows raised, nodding his head, "was your silver pelts. I got that tip right out of the Exchange. If I can control the silvers, I've . . . we've got it made. And that's where you figure!"

Webb nodded in a sort of trance. He was trying to keep two lines of thought going, and at the same time listen to Savote. He noticed Milt reach out a restraining hand.

"Listen, Rich, cut the kid a deal. Don't tip the caper."

"Shut up," snapped Savote. "You goofed this fix for me once. I'll handle it now." He leaned back, smiling, but the white knuckles gripping the Magnum belied his apparent ease. The words continued to pour out. "I like you, Webb. You don't say much . . . here's how it will go . . . twenty bucks for every silver. You had thirty blankets in that last shipment. That'd been better than half a grand . . . six hundred . . . for you! A cute deal, too. Your game ranger friend couldn't hook you up. It's as clean as . . ."

140

Savote threw back his head to blow a plume of smoke into the air, and suddenly he froze, then almost in one motion he raised his Magnum and fired.

No one had seen the lone mallard fly in. The exploding express shell in the Magnum brought it down, spinning on a broken wing. It plopped into the soft sand near the pit. The wounded bird struggled up and waddled toward the water, as Webb alerted Champ.

"Hold the dog," snapped Savote, flicking the autoloader to his shoulder and smiling with a greedy look in his eyes that revolted Webb. The double blast from the lowered muzzle drove the boy back. The duck disappeared, shredded by the express loads, and only a raw gash was left in the sand where the mallard had been a moment before.

"Man!" grunted Savote, chewing his cigar vigorously. "This is a killer! This gun's got power! That's what I like. Plenty power!"

Webb was seeing a different Savote from the one he had up to now. The light eyes were almost colorless under the down-drawn brows. The tightly-clamped cigar stretched the mouth grotesquely to one side as the man rolled and chewed it.

"Let's cut the yakking, Webb. You've heard the deal. Where do you plan on putting the skins so that we can pick them up?" Savote tried to smile, but it was poorly managed, and Webb recognized it for the mask it was intended to be.

Now the confusion had cleared in the boy's mind. He made his decision and shook his head.

"It's no deal," he said clearly, pulling off the mitten with the heater, and stripping off the down jacket. His mouth was dry, but he went on, "I'm quitting, too.

141

You don't have to pay me, for Champ or for the blind."

He started to pick up his repeater, but Savote put his hand on the gun.

There was an ominous silence in the blind.

Webb sensed Milt moving around behind him. In the distance, a motor sounded, puttering first and then rising to a roar as the boatman advanced the throttle.

Savote cursed vilely. "What's that stupid . . ."

"Rich, you shot the signal—killing that mallard—you didn't mean to, but you did. One and two quick ones. You told Bango to get over here, quick, when he heard it." Milt's face was pale and his eyes were slits.

Webb's heart crowded into his tightening throat. Perspiration started from his temples, even though he stood in the cold wind with his jacket in his hand.

14.

WEBB'S LABRADOR PROVES UP

Webb watched as Savote coolly picked up the repeating shotgun and ejected the shells, then laid it out of his reach. The man spat out his chewed cigar butt and took the wrapper off a fresh one. Slowly, methodically, he prepared it for lighting, occasionally glancing sidewise at the boy. They were cold, calculating surveys.

"Gather up the gear," he said finally to Milt. The tone was flat, the deliberateness forced. "Take it down and have Bango get the boats. Tell him I said so."

Savote blew a plume of smoke into the air and watched it being whipped away by the wind. Webb saw the cold eyes change, mirroring a new thought.

"Just haul the gear down . . . then come back and watch him. I'll talk to Bango."

Webb felt faint when he realized the implication in Savote's veiled glances and in the clipped and brittle words. He felt like running, even considered snatching the Magnum. Then he knew it was too late. Savote casually shifted his position, bringing the muzzle into alignment with Webb's belt buckle. The man's face became a mask.

The only visible movement now was the cigar, which began to turn over and over in the slowly-grinding jaws.

Webb started to speak. Savote waved the gun.

"Shut up! It's too late."

Webb's mind flew from one idea to another. He looked down at Champ, lying half-asleep at his feet. Now he wished he had trained the dog to fight on command, to charge, to . . . but Champ had only been trained to retrieve, he concluded his desperate thoughts.

He looked beyond Savote and saw that Bango had beached his boat and that Milt was talking to him. Then Milt came back.

"Get down in the blind," Savote ordered Webb. "Milt, sit down, make it look natural. Someone might come along before dark." Savote picked up Webb's shotgun and walked away.

Down in the blind, Webb couldn't see what was going on beyond the rim. Milt sat on the edge, holding the shotgun on him.

"What are you going to do?" Webb managed to ask.

The dapper man shook his head resignedly. "The boss is funny—you can't tell—when you cross him." Then Milt wouldn't talk any more, in spite of Webb's repeated questions, except to say, "You saw the duck; he's that way."

The motors of the boats Webb had hidden in the tules were started, as each was brought to the shore of the island, near the blind. Then the boy heard Savote call, "Okay, walk him down here."

Webb watched as Bango carried out Savote's plan. The big man loaded and shot the boy's gun into the air. Then, tossing the discharged weapon into Webb's boat, he climbed in and started the motor. Milt started the other boat and followed Bango into midstream. There they brought the boats parallel to each other and headed them upstream. Bango climbed into Milt's boat, reached over and opened the throttle of Webb's motor. The released boat ran straight up the river for a ways, then began slowly curving toward the California shore.

Webb's head throbbed with a sudden understanding of Savote's plan. He felt stiff, paralyzed.

"Put a rope on the dog, Milt. I want him."

The Labrador went meekly enough, and now Webb realized how cleverly Savote had planned it all, even to feeding Champ to win his trust.

Bango objected, "Hadn't you better forget that pot-licker?"

"I want him," repeated Savote with a warning note in his voice. "I'm flying out of Needles tonight." He took his cigar out of his mouth and gestured. "I'll give the orders; you take 'em. Get it?"

Milt, standing behind Savote, shook his head, but Bango nodded agreement. So the smaller man shrugged his shoulders.

"Give us thirty minutes . . . then just before dark . . . We'll see you a mile or so above Needles."

Savote never gave Webb another look, but the boy watched the heavy jaw working as it chewed another cigar into bits. Nothing would change his mind now, no hope of mercy from him.

Webb looked at Bango. The tank boss stared back with a leering grin and continued to shift a huge wad of tobacco in his cheek. Then, wiping his stained mouth with one dirty hand, he sat down slowly on the prow of his beached boat, holding a shotgun carelessly across his massive thighs, which were too big for the hip boots he wore. The unfastened tops were only partly pulled up.

Savote got into the boat and held the rope to which Champ was tied. Milt pushed off and started the motor. As the boat drew away, Champ whined anxiously and looked back. Webb saw Savote take a shorter grip on the rope and form a loop with which he struck the dog.

"Down," commanded Savote. But Champ continued to pull, then attempted to jump out of the boat as it picked up speed.

Webb watched miserably as it got farther and farther away and Champ fought harder. The boy almost cried out as Savote stood up, his arm rising and falling repeatedly. Just before the boat disappeared, Webb saw Champ whirl from trying to get out of the boat. The retriever faced Savote in the prow. Then the boat disappeared in the swiftly-gathering dusk. Webb shut his eyes and pressed his lips together, tight.

Bango spat into the wet sand in front of Webb's feet, spattering the boy's shoes.

"Too bad the boss got on a talking jag. He spilled the whole setup, then natcherly he couldn't let you go." The man's grin was one of malicious pleasure.

Webb tried to speak, but he couldn't. His tongue lay dry in his mouth. The muscles tightened and cramped in his neck and stomach. He would have cried out if he had been able.

Bango shifted his weight on the boat and moved his feet. One boot top slid down, turning inside out and trailing in the water. Webb wondered dully why he should notice such small details, but there was nothing he could do about the big problem. He stared as if hypnotized at the muzzle of the shotgun, its open end only a few inches from the wet mud.

Bango rolled the cud in his mouth and spat again, this

146

time right on Webb's feet. Then he laughed hugely. "Too bad we ain't in the bullpen, Dodge. I'd have you cleanin' the floor!" Again he roared, throwing back his head and opening his mouth so you could see the cud lying on his tongue. The muzzle of the shotgun was almost touching the water-washed silt.

Webb hoped the desperate idea that flashed into his mind didn't show on his face!

Bango laughed again. "I always like to see punks like you cleanin' up the floor." He spat again, this time on Webb's legs, and this time he guffawed even louder, hitting his thigh with one hand and rocking with amusement.

It was then that Webb jumped, grabbing the carelessly-held gun and jamming its muzzle deep into the mud. He jerked at the gun before Bango could recover, pulling the man forward and stepping on the trailing boot top at the same time.

The big man fell forward, dragging Webb down. Bango's tremendous strength was too much for the boy. He felt the gun barrel twist from his grasp. Bango raised it to strike, and Webb covered his head with his arms. There was a shattering noise, but he felt nothing, so he raised his eyes. The gun barrel had exploded when Bango's movement had discharged the gun, Webb thought, splitting from breech to muzzle. The man dropped the gun, his left hand, which had been on the forepiece, spurting blood. His right hand drew back as Webb moved backward. The boy saw it coming; it sloughed into his face.

He rolled into the water and jerked up his head in time to meet Bango's booted foot so it glanced off his skull. Then the muddy water, the darkening sky and the figure of Bango rising in front of him all disappeared in a rush of blackness.

147

A wind seemed to be pressing Webb, a rushing wind carrying rain with it. The rain came in sheets, strangling sheets that crashed on him. He felt unable to move, even when the water cascaded over him.

It was funny, the rain seemed to be coming from underneath, blowing upward into his nose and mouth. He gasped for air—and then he knew where he was: draped over the prow of Bango's speeding boat! The rising spray from the knifing prow was washing over his head.

When he gained consciousness and gulped air, the boy felt a jab in the ribs and Bango pushed him off with an oar. He slid into the river, limp as a sack of sand, and the water closed over him as he felt the blade of the oar push him down.

His head throbbed. His body ached. For a moment he wanted desperately to just sink deep. Then the cold water shocked him to full consciousness. He felt his feet drag bottom and he struggled up.

149

Fortunately for Webb, the Colorado River, in its main channel, is a roiling mass, chewing at the bottom, its clearness clouded with sand and silt. So, in the twilight, Bango missed the boy in the turbid water.

Webb began to stroke feebly, the current washing him along, the churning, boiling water holding him up. After what seemed an endless time, unreal and nightmarish, he felt himself roll onto something solid. He finally realized that he had come to rest on a gilhooly, one of the thousands of hidden, moving sandbars. He struggled to crawl up at just about the same time that Bango made his last circle a short fifty yards away and straightened out his course to run downstream.

Then Webb collapsed and his head fell forward into the few inches of water washing over the bar. He choked and turned enough to allow him to breathe.

It was some time before strength returned to him. It came in shivering waves, and at last he made himself move, crawling up on the bar.

The dark was settling fast. Webb looked around, trying to orient himself. The California shore was a black line on the still visible horizon, which meant the Arizona side was closer. He had to shift his weight, for the rapidly-running river ate the sand away from under his knees. Then he struggled to his feet. A cold wind ate at his strength, so he lowered himself to the water again.

He felt the silt bar dissolve under his hands and knees as the river chewed out the supporting sand and spewed it up. Wherever he touched the bar the river sucked it away.

Webb's head sagged as he realized his predicament. The bar was dissolving under him; soon he would have to swim, and he felt unequal to the task. The Colorado flowed by, silt-laden and quiet, except for a soft, inviting whispering, constantly gnawing at the bar.

At first Webb thought it was just the throbbing in his head. Then he realized that the pounding in his ears was the distant barking of a dog. It was a moment before he recognized Champ's voice!

A surge of strength flowed through the boy's body. He raised his head and whistled, sharp, shrill—twice. The effort cost him precious energy, but in another minute or so he whistled again. Each time he did so—two blasts was the signal he always used to summon Champ—he felt new confidence, new hope.

When the big dog finally splashed up out of the dark water onto the bar, wriggling with delight, Webb broke into a hoarse cry and hugged him, rubbing his wet coat and half-laughing as he said, "Champ! Ol' boy!" over and over. When his hands went over the dog, the boy discovered a piece of rope still trailing from his neck, but there were no injuries, as far as he could tell.

The dog's warm, wet tongue on his face, and the activity of petting him, warmed Webb, and the resilient young strength started to flow back into his arms and legs. His mind cleared and he began to realize what he must do. He stumbled to his feet, holding onto the dog for steadying, knowing he must keep his footing on the melting gilhooly.

He tried to untie his shoestrings, but finally had to cut them with the sheath knife which was still on his belt. He tied the shoes together and hung them around his neck. Next, he stripped off his binding leather jacket and let it float away.

Then he stood up and faced the Arizona shore, waved his arm to the Labrador and said, "Go! Go! Champ, go!"

The dog looked at him questioningly. At the second command, the big retriever entered the water.

Webb, heart in his throat, looped the short rope around his hand and slid into the water alongside the dog, who was already swimming.

When Champ first felt the weight on his neck, he hesitated. Webb, with great effort, rose in the water, waved his arm forward and repeated, "Go! Go!" At this, the dog settled down, swimming powerfully, and as the rope tightened, Webb stroked with his free arm, kicking with his feet as hard as he could. He had difficulty keeping the dog headed directly across the river. Champ wanted to swing upstream and swim directly against the current.

Webb felt a flood of gratitude for the dog swimming steadily beside him. The boy's stretched left arm lay alongside the retriever's thick body, and he could feel the muscles roll in the powerful shoulders. He remembered Judge Schaulkler's story of how Labradors had been developed, and felt grateful pride for the hidden strengths and the loyalty bred into this wonderful friend of his.

Then, Champ coughed and slackened his speed. Webb realized that the rope and his weight were too much for the dog, and for a moment fear clutched him like the dark water, then he had a desperate inspiration. He grasped the labrador's thick, tapering tail, taking a firm hold with his right hand, then shouted again, "Go! Go!"

Once more Champ plowed through the water, as strongly as before, towing the boy behind him.

Webb drew on every reserve for strength, stroking mightily with his free arm and kicking with his feet. Would they make it? He was sobbing for breath and his chest was raw with pain.

Finally the silhouette of Champ's head disappeared

against the shadow of rising trees and tules. Webb sensed the dog climbing, and his own hands and feet felt the sticky mud of the Arizona bank.

Their combined all-out effort had been enough! He dragged himself up, grasping the fringing willows and worming through them, to drop on dry ground. The last thing he remembered was Champ's warm breath on his cheek and the big tongue licking, licking at his face.

15.

WEBB GOES IT ALONE

Webb braked Brant's truck on the steep grade. Far, far
below, the Colorado River flowed blue and clear through
a deep canyon. It came out of a gorge to the right, swung
toward them and then away.

"That bend, that's Willow Beach," he said to Tom.

The old trapper leaned forward to look. "Is that where
we're goin' to set up camp, in that sand and boulder wash?"
he complained.

Webb had to laugh, in spite of his puffed and sore lips,
the result of Bango's kick. Tom was his usual self. The
laugh sent a sharp pain around Webb's ribs and to his
back. He grimaced. Tom looked at him sharply.

"Sure you're ready to start trappin' again?" he asked
with concern. "Doc said you shoulda laid in a day or two
yet."

Webb shook his head. "Brant needs this beaver project
put over, and all the pelts we can stretch will help do it.
We've lost too much time as it is."

Tom blinked his eye and nodded agreement to that.

A horn tooted behind them and Webb knew the game ranger had caught up. In his rear-vision mirror he could now see the patrol car, with Brant's boat and motor trailed behind. This was now to be Webb's outfit, since his craft had been badly wrecked when it smashed into a gravel bank while traveling at full speed.

Webb's fingers delicately explored the healing cuts and bruises around the left side of his face and head. Bango had really given him a beating! Webb clamped his teeth together, making a new and deep resolve; this beaver-trapping project was going to be put over if he had anything to do with it. Poor-pay job or no, Webb knew he was now dedicated to helping Brant make it go.

The game ranger had visited him often during his days in the hospital. Webb had argued that there was nothing wrong that time wouldn't cure, but the doctors had insisted on holding him for observation. Now the boy was glad it had happened just that way, for during his stay Brant had told him about the developments within the game department.

He could recall Brant's exact words: "Maybe it's just a dream, but here's what I would like to do. I want to make the Director and the Commissioners realize that they need a division of fur conservation within the department.

"I believe they'll see it my way, if I can make this beaver-trapping project pay off, money-wise.

"Up to now, no one has realized we had as many beaver over here on the river as we do—nobody except the poachers, and you and I. And I wouldn't have known about it if it hadn't been for you."

Webb remembered how the game ranger had leaned over the foot of the hospital bed and looked past him into nowhere, while he told of his dream.

155

"This whole country had beaver in it. All the little streams coming off the Mogollon Rim, the creeks in the Tonto Basin and on the Apache Indian Reservation—they all had beaver. Even the Salt River and the Gila had beaver. James Ohio Pattie, one of the first to trap this country, took beaver.

"But all these streams have just a few beaver on them now—they are almost exterminated."

"Where did the beaver come from—the ones here on the river—if they were all trapped out?" Webb had asked then.

"It's my guess they came down the river out of the Grand Canyon, where the early day trappers and the poachers who came later, couldn't get at them."

That sounded sensible to Webb. Brant had continued, "I'd like to put beaver back on all those streams where they once lived."

"How?" asked Webb, caught up in Brant's dreaming.

"Live-trap them and haul them overland with a truck." Brant grinned, but Webb noticed how the determined jaw of the ranger slid forward a bit farther, in spite of the easy smile. "But first this trapping project has got to pay off," he went on. "Your knock-down-and-drag-out with those contrabanders and Bango jarred the game department, even if it didn't do you any good. Those fellows in the state office thought I was having a nightmare when I told them about your experience.

"And the size of those checks coming from the Seattle Fur Exchange for the first shipments of beaver pelts helped to open their eyes." Brant had smiled wryly, then turned serious again. "Webb, I've got a very good chance of getting this Division of Fur Conservation set up. If I do, how about your working for me? You could make yourself a stake and then go on to college . . . and from there, you're on your way up in this conservation business! How about that?"

It was after this visit of Brant's that Webb had really revised his thinking. The ranger needed him; wanted him. He knew he was an important part of the man's hopes, and that he had a chance to be a part of a big, exciting new development. The boy was surprised to discover how badly he wanted to have Brant succeed, and how anxious he now was to help the ranger to do it.

Webb felt a hand on his knee. Tom gripped it just in time to wake the boy up to the fact that the car was rolling, and would have gone right out on the sandy bar and into the Colorado River!

He slammed on the brakes and skidded to a stop, exclaiming, "Wow! I must have been dreaming."

"Whaddaya mean, 'must have been'! You *were!*" the old man grumbled, opening the door so Champ could jump out.

Webb alighted somewhat awkwardly. His back and ribs were stiff, but he knew he would loosen up if he moved around a little.

Brant pulled up behind and got out of the patrol car.

"Let's set up the camp first," he suggested, "and then launch the boat and take a run up and down the river and look over the trapping prospects."

The three of them fell on the work and in only a matter of minutes they had the tent set up, the gear stowed and the boat launched.

"You'd better take the motor, Webb," said the game ranger, shoving the boat out and holding the prow while the others climbed in. "I'd like to go up through Ring Bolt Rapids and then, if we have time, down to Roaring Rapids and below. There's some bad water in Crane's Nest, and they tell me the Ring Bolt is a regular Coney Island roller-coaster."

"They're pretty rough," admitted Webb. "I haven't been through the Ring Bolt, just up to the tail, once. The Ring Bolt and Roaring Rapids are the worst below Hoover Dam. Crane's Nest is next. The rest don't amount to much."

The game ranger grunted as he pushed the boat off into the eddy forming in the bend below Willow Beach. "I thought you'd had more experience running rapids than I have, which is next to nothing," he said.

Webb pulled the starting cord, and the motor began its steady puttering. He breathed the motor a few times, accelerating and decelerating, to clear out the carburetor and cylinder heads, then he slowly shoved the throttle over to full speed.

Brant looked around questioningly. Webb cocked his head and listened. The motor responded to the extra fuel with a smooth, powerful roar. The boy looked up at the ranger and grinned, winked an eye to show satisfaction. It was a sweet sound, the thunder of a well-functioning outboard! The boat climbed up on the step with its three passengers and uneven plumes of spray flared out from each side.

Webb reached out and touched Tom, who was sitting midship. He motioned the old trapper to shift toward the outside about six inches. This trimmed the craft.

The feel of the speeding boat under him was good. He looked ahead to Champ, who was up front, sitting alongside the ranger. The dog was drinking in the clean air, catching wavering scents. As they left the beach, turning north and upstream, the canyon narrowed. Sheer cliffs pressed in, rising straight up for hundreds of feet to shut

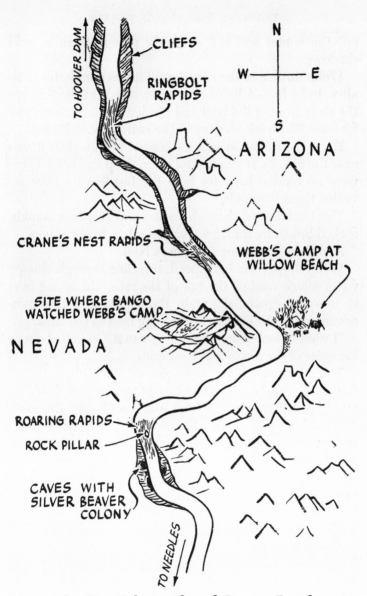

Map of the Ring Bolt Rapids and Roaring Rapids region

out the winter sun and suddenly plunge them in cold shadows.

Webb thrilled to the experience; it was wonderful to be alive, to be free. A brace of green-winged teal leaped into the air in front of the boat and headed up the canyon, and for once Webb felt no envy of the swiftly-flying birds.

Here, the Colorado was a different stream than it was near the Slough. It was crystal clear, deep and cold. There were no hidden bars, for here the fast-flowing river revealed them by rapids.

The boat flashed through Indian and Rainbow Rapids, rocked briefly by rolling water and a few frothy waves.

And then they came to Crane's Nest.

Webb dropped to half-speed, traveling through choppy water which marked the tail of the race. He swung over to move upstream alongside the rapids and thus take advantage of the quieter water lying next to the bank.

"I want to look it over before we run it," he called above the noise of the motor and the rapids.

The Colorado River here poured through a funnel formed by enormous quantities of gravel and boulders which had been pushed from a sidewash into the main canyon. This partial dam forced all the river to one side and against a sheer cliff, and through one narrow opening. Above the dike, the confined water was deep, smooth and deceptively quiet. At the lip it flowed over, looking heavy and smooth, like molten lead, thought Webb. Then it broke into increasingly larger waves, finally becoming frothy and wild, to quiet down in the choppy water he had just passed through.

He planned his approach and course. It would be just to the right, to take advantage of the eddy lying alongside the fast water, then he would whip over to the left, climb up on the crest and shoot over the lip and through the mouth, onto the quiet water above. There was only one danger. If he went too far over, to the left of the crest, the boat might be swept against the rocky walls of the cliff which rose on the other side of the rapids.

He swung the craft around, dropped downstream, and turned in the choppy water. Brant put his arm over the dog and gripped the gunnels as Webb opened the throttle. Tom took his tight hold on the boat seat. Everything was ready for the try!

The craft skittered upstream, riding high on the rough water. Webb jockeyed it close to the rapids, but not into the full force of the current. Then, at the exact instant, he pulled the tiller to the right, swerving the boat up onto the lip. It hung there a moment, throbbing like a thing alive, breasting the full sweep of the river which was fighting to press it back. Webb heard the motor snarl angrily, then surge ahead.

They slid onto the smooth, mirror-like water. Just above the rapids, off to the left and on the Nevada side, a dead but still brave cottonwood tree stood on a small patch of ground. A bevy of blue herons was perched in the gaunt limbs festooned with ragged nests.

Brant waved toward the landmark for which the rapids were named as the boat picked up speed again.

When Webb saw the Ring Bolt Rapids for the second time in his life, he knew that Crane's Nest was a mere riffle. Here was bad water!

Taking advantage of the eddy lying alongside the roaring water for his initial approach, he got close enough so he and Brant could look it over. As at Crane's Nest, a deposit of boulders coming out of a side canyon had formed a partial dike across the channel. The river behind the dike was glass-smooth, but it became a seething, tearing, tumbling force after its release through the break in the natural dam. The waves were twice as high as at Crane's Nest. Their thundering drowned out the roar of the motor.

Brant turned to shout, but Webb shook his head; he couldn't even hear the game ranger's voice. He turned downstream, and soon they were where they could talk.

"What do you think?" shouted Webb.

Brant's eyes shone with suppressed excitement; his face was wet with spray. Webb could see that running the Ring Bolt was a challenge to the doughty ranger, even before he yelled, "We've got a good boat, let's take it on for a round!"

"How about you, Tom?"

"It's goin' t' be a rough ride, but let 'er buck."

So Webb pushed the throttle over to three-quarters speed and moved up alongside the famous Ring Bolt for another survey. It was truly a formidable barrier to the trip upriver.

He planned his route to take full advantage of all the quieter water before being forced up onto the crest of the race itself. He swung in close to the rapids and peered down in the water for possible boulders or rocks which might shear a propeller pin on his approach. The way appeared to be clear.

He started the preliminary circle, going downstream. As he swung the boat around and opened the throttle, Brant turned. A wide smile lit his face, his set teeth gleamed and he gripped his hands over his head.

The boat rocketed forward from the full thrust of the propeller. Under Webb's skilled hand, it responded to every deflection on the tiller. It squirmed through the froth. It bucked and pitched when it hit the rough water.

Webb waited until the last possible moment, then swung the prow over. It knifed through the spray and into the racing water pouring through the break in the rocky dike. For a moment the boat twisted, undecided which way to go. Webb fought to correct the drift, swung the stern behind the prow. Then they were poised on the lip. There they hung, almost motionless, the motor snarling frustration.

All three men leaned forward, trying by sheer will to push the boat over the hump. It faltered, losing a few inches, then gaining again.

To Webb it was exhilarating. Brant shot a grin over his shoulder and made a couple of expressive left jabs. Tom, unused to the violence of roaring water like this, showed some fear. His hands were white with tension as he gripped the boat seat.

The Ring Bolt won!

Slowly, at first, the boat gave way. Webb pushed the tiller over, snapping it around. They slid down the chute to hit the first wave with a resounding and jolting smash.

As they hit, the old trapper lost his grip and pitched forward into the bottom of the boat. Webb's eyes were lifted to the rapids ahead and he didn't dare relax, but he felt a stab of fear—Tom was hurt! Brant reached behind and caught the old man's coat in a tight grip as the boat pitched into the second wave. But Tom was caught unprepared for the jar, and his head snapped forward again, hitting the back of the forward seat. Webb saw the old man's hand flash up to cover his good eye, but too late! It came away dripping with blood.

Webb could only hope to bring them safely through the rapids. He saw his chance and slid out onto a smooth eddy. Tom raised his head.

Then Webb could see that the skin was cut deep along the brow. The blood was flowing freely, blinding the one good eye. Tom tried to wipe away the blood.

Brant turned to examine the eye, and the old trapper wavered on the verge of fainting.

Webb knew real fear then. He watched Brant's serious face for its first telltale expression, and felt a great relief as the ranger spoke reassuringly to Tom.

"Just a cut on the eyebrow—but a deep one. You'll have to have some stitches. It's a couple of inches long, too."

The old trapper shook his head to clear it, and glared at the roaring Ring Bolt.

"That's sure enough a ringtailin' son-of-a-gun!" he said belligerently. "But I wouldn'ta missed it!"

After another look at Tom's eye, Brant said, "Listen, old-timer, we'd better get right back to camp and then you go with me to Kingman. We've got to take care of that cut."

The downstream run to Willow Beach was made quickly. It was then that the other two knew that Tom was really hurt worse than he'd admit. He needed help to get into Brant's car. The ranger shut the door and turned quickly to Webb.

"You'll have to go it alone. Can do?"

"You bet," Webb said with conviction. "I'll take care of it. You keep me in grub and pick up the pelts. I'll do the rest."

The ranger's admiration was on his face and in his voice as he gave the boy a pat on the back.

"We will if you feel that way about it, Kid."

Tom stirred in the car and mumbled, "Flesh them pelts clean, Webb, or I'll come back an' take the hide offa *you*."

Webb laughed, encouraged. The old boy still had plenty of spirit.

As Brant's car pulled up the steep grade, Webb felt a cold muzzle forcing its way into his hand.

"Job's all ours, now, Champ!" he said aloud as he fondled the soft ears.

While Webb was alone,

Webb laughed, encouraged. The old boy still had had plenty

Blondie's ear pull

"Let's all out, now. Gimmy" he said aloud as he fondled the soft fur.

16.

ROARING RAPIDS REVEAL A SECRET

The first day Webb was alone, he loaded his boat with trapping gear and made a run down the river. The thought of exploring Roaring Rapids intrigued him.

Here below Willow Beach, the mountains were set back from the river bank. There were flats of land covered with willows and studded with occasional cottonwoods. The Colorado was wide, smooth and gentle-flowing.

Everywhere Webb looked, he saw signs of beaver: cuttings, slides and other evidences of the furbearers. Now that he was alone, he would have to organize his work carefully, if he was to get it all done. So, he began planning his work day, running his traps in the morning and skinning and stretching and fleshing pelts in the afternoon.

The thunder of the racing, turbulent water of Roaring Rapids was a warning to him. While he was still a long way upstream from the bad water, he dropped the speed of his boat and swung it around to head back the way he had come. Then he adjusted the throttle so that the forward speed of the boat was balanced by the current. Thus,

166

he was slowly carried backward toward the lip of the rapids. From this position he could look over the dangerous water.

He could see that Roaring Rapids, like the others, had been caused by deposits of floods pouring into the channel from two side canyons. It was a long stretch of rough water, more dangerous than the Ring Bolt, because it was shallower. The white water told him that reefs of boulders lay close to the surface.

A hundred yards or so downstream from the lip, a huge, massive pillar of rock rose out of the middle of the rapids. Webb could see that two thirds of the rapids spilled around the west side, while a third of it poured around to the east.

The best run appeared to be just to the right of the big rocky pillar.

He opened the throttle and headed upstream, swinging wide and gaining speed. He ordered Champ off the deck and into the bottom of the boat, then he sped over the lip to shoot out onto the tongue. His line of travel was to the right of the crest, which centered on the rock pillar.

The lightly-laden boat bucked and pitched like a chip, shooting off one wave to crash onto the next. Webb felt as if he were half flying. As he neared the barrier, he first intended to ride the current, but seeing how close it brought him to the pillar, he carefully guided the boat a couple of feet to the right.

As he shot by the pillar, he felt, rather than heard, his propeller hit an underwater obstacle, but he drew a breath of relief when he realized no damage had been done. He was puzzled, however, and swung sharply to the left, coming up behind the rock and in the shelter of the eddy. The rapids roared angrily by on each side.

167

Webb studied the swirling water, which alternately cleared, then frothed and boiled. It was perhaps five minutes before he saw the slender comb of thin spires projecting upward from the green depths. The comb ran out from the pillar a dozen feet. On his run he had just missed clearing the end of it; apparently his stabilizing fin had just ticked the last spire!

Webb felt a wave of fear when he realized how close he had come to crashing and tearing the bottom out of his boat. If his course had been six inches closer to the pillar, it would have been disastrous. He shuddered, thinking of it.

That comb of rocks was something to remember, that was for sure!

As he watched, the water smoothed and cleared again. He got a more distinct view of the reef. Surprisingly, right next to the pillar there was a gap in the comb, just wide enough for a boat to pass through—if the boatman happened to be crazy enough to try it. This would be something like trying to shoot a .22 through a keyhole at ten yards, Webb thought, as he swung the boat back into the current.

A rock mountain loomed in front of him, several hundred yards below the rapids and on the Nevada side. He steered for an enormous cave opening at waterline and recalled that some people referred to Roaring Rapids as Cave Rapids.

As he came closer, he saw there was a deposit of driftwood in the funnel-like cavern. The opening was surprisingly big, and he ran his boat into it and tied up to the trunk of a cottonwood tree which was locked into the pile of driftwood.

Champ stuck his head down among the logs and whined.
Then Webb saw a beaver underneath . . .

The air was sickeningly sweet with the odor of beaver. As he clambered over the long-dead wood, he detected a movement below him. Champ stuck his head down among the logs and whined. Then Webb saw a beaver underneath, another and another. He whistled.

"Hey, Champ! A colony."

The beaver were all making for the safety of the water, slipping into their element and swimming down and away. As they passed into the stronger light, Webb saw that every one was the odd, light color.

"All of them silvers, every one!" he mouthed softly.

Seven beaver in all scrambled along the runway and down into the water.

Webb began thinking immediately on the problem of catching them. There was no way for him to get at the beavers' runway because of the deposit of driftwood. Then the thought occurred to him—the beaver had to go out to eat, to swim either up- or downstream to the patches of willows.

That's where he would set his traps.

It was noon before he got back to Willow Beach, and it was almost dark before he'd finished making his sets above the camp.

The next day saw a changed Webb. He was up before dawn, and well down the river by daylight. There he ran the traps, reset them and returned to Willow Beach with his catch. He skinned the beaver, fleshed and stretched the pelts before noon. In the afternoon, he went upstream, repeating his routine of the morning.

This became his daily pattern. He didn't even notice just when the soreness left his body. It wasn't many days before he began removing cured pelts from the frames.

170

He built a rack for these, and it was surprising how fast they began to accumulate. It worked out better than he had expected. He found he could catch more beaver with fewer traps because, in this end of the Colorado, the food was concentrated on flats between the cliffs.

"Makes the beaver come to us, Champ, instead of us having to hunt them." He spoke to the dog as if he were old Tom, and Champ blinked his amber eyes as if he understood.

By tightening up his routine and thinking out some short cuts, Webb found he had some free time. He began taking his shotgun along on his trips downriver, where the canyon was more open and where he potholed a few mallards. There he worked the Labrador through some retrieving problems.

He also met the challenge of the Ring Bolt and ran it, this time without incident and quite successfully.

"No trick at all," he commented to Champ when they slid out on the smooth water above, "At least, not with an empty boat."

Running the Ring Bolt made him anxious to know how Tom was getting along. He had been working so hard he had almost forgotten to keep track of the time. He tried to figure it out and found he couldn't even remember what day it was.

"Let's see," he said, driving the boat onto a sandbank in a quiet eddy. He shut off the motor and took a screwdriver from his repair kit. He knew he had all but eleven of the hundred stretchers filled with curing pelts.

"That's eighty-nine curing," he mused.

Then, mentally, he totaled the already cured and stacked pelts, "Eight dark ones, and . . . golleee . . . twenty-one silvers, Champ! Over a thousand dollars' worth of silvers already!" The dog cocked his head, listening to his master's strange mutterings.

Webb felt an intense glow of pride; every pelt was stretched round and tight as a drum head. They were clean, too, each one fleshed smooth and each had dried as white as paper.

With the screwdriver, he scratched furiously on the worktable, making the figures 8—21—89 and added them.

"Hundred and eighteen," he said aloud. Then he looked up thoughtfully, and absently put the screwdriver in his mouth, like a pencil. He sputtered, spitting out the gasoline and oil taste, but this didn't delay his thinking. "About nine a day."

He divided the total by nine. "Gee, thirteen or fourteen days—about two weeks—since Tom was hurt!"

This realization left him worried. The old trapper must have been hurt worse than they had known, otherwise Brant would have brought him back by now.

"Maybe they're at the Beach now," the boy said to Champ, voicing the thought as it occurred. He pushed the boat off the bar and started the motor. The ten- to fifteen-mile-an-hour current added greatly to the speed of his boat. He took every advantage of it. As he neared the Beach, he became anxious with the rising hope that Brant would be there with Tom.

The Beach was quiet. The still-drying beaver pelts, stretched on steel hoops, hung idly in the shade of the willow ramada he had built.

Webb felt sharp disappointment.

Three more long days passed. If it hadn't been for two trout that he caught and the teal and canvasback that fell to his shotgun, he would have become meat-hungry. He had tired of the beaver steaks and stews that he and Tom

172

had often prepared, and which he had eaten with relish, at first. Only Champ enjoyed the rich, red meat now.

At noon of the fourth day, Webb's keen eyes caught the glint of sun on polished metal as he rounded the bend, coming back from his morning trip to Roaring Rapids.

It was Brant's car.

"Where's Tom?" Webb asked as soon as he turned off the motor and coasted onto the Beach.

Brant shook his head. "That cut was worse than I thought. Well, the cut itself wasn't so bad; it was the jolt he got. That, and his age, knocked him over for a count." Brant looked around at the neat camp and down into the boat, then up at Webb. "You're really working, aren't you, boy! That's six this morning, five silvers and a black one. And you've got fifty-four ready to ship."

"Never mind the beaver—what about Tom?"

The ranger chuckled. "Him? He'll do all right—if they can keep him down. The doc wants him to stay quiet another week, but you know what a stubborn old coot he is! They want a close check on the eye. That bump knocked a splinter of bone off the brow and drove it back under. A chip fracture; but he's doing all right now." Brant gave the boy a friendly jab in the shoulder. "*He's* worrying about *you,* and how you're getting along!"

Webb gave the ranger a slow smile, and a warm feeling filled him. He liked knowing that the cantankerous trapper was thinking of him. "I've been busy," he admitted. "When you go back, I want to send him a trout. I've caught some dandies here."

Brant nodded approvingly. "Yes, you have been in there slugging, I can see that. But, Webb, I can't take that fish, nor the pelts you have ready. I'm going the other way."

"What do you mean?"

"I only had time to bring you some chuck and drop it off. We've got a tip some bighorn sheep poachers are hunting in Grand Wash, on the north side of Lake Mead." Brant grimaced ruefully. "You ought to know the game department by now, Webb. They give big game law violations the edge over everything else. I've got to drop everything and check on that. If I don't have any luck catching the trophy hunters, I'll be back in about a week. If I catch the poachers, it may be two weeks or more, because I'll have to cite them into court and prepare a case against them."

Webb frowned and shook his head. "And leave all these pelts here with me?" he questioned. "Gee, Brant, I've got over two thousand dollars' worth of cured pelts here now! And more coming up every day."

Brant shrugged his shoulders. "They're as safe here as they would be locked in the back of my car, Webb, and they'll keep a lot better."

Webb walked around in a circle. The idea of keeping all these valuable pelts so long made him nervous.

"Relax, relax," said the ranger. "Don't worry about it. No one knows you're in here trapping beaver; this camp is pretty well hidden from river traffic."

Webb shook his head. "I don't know. . . . Bango and those hot-fur dealers might have us spotted, and if I . . . if they . . ." He faltered and looked at the ground while he smoothed the sand with the sole of one boot.

"Come on, give out. What's on your mind?"

"Well, heck, Brant, they'd hijack the furs in a minute if they knew where they were. Then you'd think . . . everybody, including Judge Schaulkler, would think I made a deal!"

"Don't ever think it, Webb. I'd believe you, and I think

I can promise you the judge would, too. Anyway, those contrabanders have probably left the country. We've had a pick-up order out to the police in Needles, but they haven't seen them. This territory just got too hot for them!"

"You don't know that tank boss . . . or Rich Savote, either, Brant! They'll do anything, if there's money in it. Believe me."

Brant rubbed his jaw thoughtfully. "Well, here's an idea,

175

then. They know now that you won't deal with them, so the only thing left for them to try is to steal the furs. If there aren't any, you have nothing to fear. So—take them out and hide them somewhere!"

Webb's face brightened. "I think I know the place—the cave at the end of Roaring Rapids."

"Yes . . ." Brant paused, thinking. "But let's see if there's anything against it: you'd have to run the rapids with a boat full of furs; they would be a long way from camp; it is probably a moist place, being down on the river. I don't know . . . I'd suggest a ledge—a high and dry ledge, closer to camp . . . a place you could watch."

"Sure." The suggestion made sense to Webb. He looked up the slope behind camp. "There's a ledge up there, and there's a prospector's hole in one end of it. That would be just the place. It's shady and airy, if we don't put them too far back in the tunnel. There's only one thing wrong with it; there might be some rats or mice there."

Brant nodded. "Sounds okay. Why not build a platform and either sling it from the ceiling on wires or set it up on stake legs, flanged by tin? I'll help you, but let's hurry. I've got to start rolling and get into camp by dark."

"You go ahead," Webb said. "I can do it."

Brant looked around at the surrounding country. Then his usually twinkling brown eyes half-closed, and he glanced back at the boy, saying thoughtfully, "You know, you might be right. It might be smart business to move those pelts up to the ledge after dark. It just might be that someone is watching this camp." Then he added a little sheepishly, "I think we're both getting all spooked over nothing, but then again, it won't cost anything to be a little smart."

That thought hadn't occurred to Webb—that his camp

176

might be watched! His eyes swept the horizon. He could see up the Colorado as it ran toward his camp, and down the river as it flowed away. Inside the bend, directly across from him, were a trio of peaks rising in a triangle, each connected to the other by a joining ridge. One of them towered above the camp. Webb looked up at the escarpment crowning the top. Two ospreys were sailing back and forth over the promontory, watching the river below.

Webb felt Brant's hand on his arm. "I've just got to get up the road," he said. "I put all the food in your tent. The butter, bacon and eggs are in the can in the river."

The two walked together to Brant's car. The ranger got in and closed the door, then he leaned out. "Well, you've got it, my boy, take good care of it."

"I will, I sure will." Webb nodded. Suddenly he leaned down and scratched Champ's ear, obviously seeking words to express a thought. "Brant, what's the judge doing about Champ?"

"What do you mean?"

"About those dots in his ears. Is he trying to trace them, to find out if Champ's registered?"

"Well . . . yes, he is . . . was, I mean. He was going to write to the American Kennel Club, but then he found out about the Labrador Retriever Club. He thought that would be the best way to run down Champ's ownership and pedigree."

Despair clouded Webb's face, then it gave way to his rising anger as he said, "Why can't he leave things alone, just forget it?"

Brant opened the car door and got out again, grasping Webb by the shoulders and turning him around.

"Listen to me before you criticize the judge. He was doing what he thought was right. But I talked it over with him and he could see it a little differently." There was an expression in the officer's eyes that Webb couldn't read. Brant said no more for a moment, then he took his hands down and got out his pipe and began filling it, so the boy couldn't see his eyes. In a little while he went on speaking, "Webb, you'll remember when you first found that pup, and I came around to talk to you?"

Webb waited to get his features under control, then he nodded.

"Remember Mercer, the hunter that was with me on that first visit," Brant continued. "He always insisted he knew that Champ belonged to a fellow we both knew. Well, I know that same fellow—slightly—and it's my bet that when the judge gets in touch with him, we'll find out that he will never want Champ back. He always struck me as a fairly reasonable guy."

The way Brant finished the statement made Webb realize that the ranger believed and meant everything he had said. It made the boy feel better, a lot better, but he still had to pull out every word of what had been building in his mind. He found a match and lit it for Brant as he spoke in low, determined tones.

"Brant, if you want me to give up Champ, I . . ." he struggled to continue, but couldn't. Then he breathed deeply and forced the words out. "I'll do anything you say, but . . . but . . . I won't have much left, if I lose Champ."

Brant was about to speak, but he apparently choked on a lungful of smoke and had a spell of coughing. At last he managed to say, "Don't worry, Kid. We'll work it out some way."

Then he started the car and turned away to climb the long grade out of Willow Beach to the main highway.

Webb watched, and in spite of the reassurances the ranger had given him, he felt as if Champ were already in the car and going away with Brant, instead of standing, as he was, in front of his young master, holding a stick and waiting for Webb to throw it out into the river.

17.

BANGO AGAIN

During the week following Brant's visit, Webb tried to change his feelings about the Labrador, by thinking of Champ as just another dog that could easily be replaced. But, perversely, it seemed, Champ made his way even deeper into his master's affections every day.

In a black mood he himself couldn't understand, Webb tried to prove that Champ was really not as smart as everyone believed. He devised some complicated retrieving problems, telling himself he hoped to stump the dog. But Champ seemed to take a contrary delight in solving them quickly and with all the flash and flourish of a well-bred, thoroughly-disciplined retriever.

It was the seventh day, just after their midday meal, and Webb had gone with his boat to take a dummy duck across the wide, swiftly-flowing river. He hid it among the willows. Champ was eagerly waiting for him, sitting on the sand beach, just below the camp.

The dog was excited, wagging his body from just back

180

of his ears all the way to the tip of his tail. As Webb stepped ashore, the retriever leaned against him, begging to be commanded to go after the hidden block.

Webb pushed him aside with the flat of his foot. Suddenly he said, "Doggone you, if you don't cut it out, Champ, I'll be bawling around like a little kid!"

The Labrador squirmed with delight, for in spite of Webb's rude gesture and unkind words, the tone of his master's voice carried the same love and affection he'd always found in him.

Then the boy dropped to his knees and reached out, encircling the big yellow dog with his arms, just as he had in the judge's office that morning Brant had brought Champ to him.

"You darned dog, you!" Unwanted tears filmed his eyes as he thought of the possibility of having to give Champ up. The huge reservoir of lonesomeness in Webb left by the death of his parents, had been almost filled by the loyal companionship of the Labrador, whose responsiveness and sense of fun had seemed truly human to the boy. He had learned to rely on the dog, and Champ had tried his best, as only a dog can, to please his beloved young master.

Webb looked up at the blue sky outlining the brown rock promontory across the river and blinked to clear his eyes of the unwelcome tears. The osprey was there, sailing back and forth over the point, scanning the river below for a careless trout in the clear water. Watching the fish-eating hawks had become a daily pastime with Webb ever since he had discovered them that day Brant had visited the camp last.

The hawk turned in lazy circles, crossing and recrossing the edge of the escarpment crowning the towering rock. Webb had spotted his perch, high on the promontory; the roost was marked by white streaks and splashes of their droppings. The mate was there.

Champ nuzzled him to remind him there were other things to do, and he sent the Labrador across the river. The current carried the swimming dog well below the place where the block was hidden.

Webb whistled sharply, and the retriever stopped in his tracks to look back across the water. Webb waved him to the right. The dog followed the shoreline, searching in and out of the willows for the canvas dummy duck he knew Webb had hidden there. Soon he found it and plunged in the water to swim back to the beach below the camp.

Webb raised his eyes to watch the fish-hunting hawks. The same one was poised on an air current flowing up and over the promontory. Suddenly it flared and winged away. The other, perched below the rim, volplaned out from the cliff and glided off. Both birds flew away up the river.

Webb wondered if something had scared them.

Then Champ came loping up. He was stepping jauntily, proudly offering the dummy duck that had been so carefully hidden.

Webb took it, patted the dog and said, "That's all for now. We've got to set traps above the Ring Bolt this afternoon."

He had met the challenge of the thundering Ring Bolt since his first failure, and had studied the fast water and discovered a route. It wasn't easy—it was still a very rough step to the river above. Each time it was an exhilarating experience, because the boy had learned that if he didn't approach the roaring torrent at just the right angle, and if he didn't take complete advantage of the full power of his motor, and employ the full use of his boating skill, the river would turn him back every time.

Webb believed he had trapped nearly every beaver from below Roaring Rapids to Willow Beach and up the river as far as the Ring Bolt. His catch had dropped off to nothing during the last few days. The only part of the river he had not trapped was above Ring Bolt Rapids.

He remembered that nearly all of the beaver he had taken just below the Ring Bolt had been of the valuable silver variety. He had hopes that the catch above would be just as select. It would give Brant's beaver trapping project a big boost.

As his boat roared up the river with Champ standing on the deck, Webb knew that the end of the beaver trapping here was near. Perhaps a week more would finish it. He wondered what he would do then.

He knew what he wanted to do, but whether or not he could manage it now was another matter. He decided then to talk it over with Brant and Judge Schaulkler the first chance he got. . . . He wanted to go back to school, at least part-time.

The gorge above the Ring Bolt was an awesome sight. Although Webb had been up there a half-dozen times now, he never tired of it. The cliffs closed in, pressing the river tight. The river, in turn, twisted and growled at being restricted. It ran swiftly, boiling and churning in the narrow canyon, but here and there, in the sheltered coves, were banks of willows where there were many slides of the visiting beaver. It was along there that Webb set his traps.

He turned the boat south when he had finished. He had begun to do more exploring of this part of the river since the trapping work had slacked off.

At times, especially during the last few days, he had seen a few bighorn sheep on the rocky crags forming the

sides of the canyon; mostly he had seen them coming out of the side canyons to drink from the river. These rare animals, carrying the big curling horns, had interested him greatly, and he found he wanted to study them.

The next few days, while he waited for Brant's return, would give him a chance to watch this big game animal. Brant had told him the bighorns were the most desired hunting trophy of all on the North American continent, and that the Arizona Game Code provided for stiffer penalties for poaching bighorns than for any other form of illegal hunting. It didn't make sense to Webb, at first. Then he reasoned that, to some hunters, stalking and getting a bighorn in the high crags must be like fooling a flock of gunwise Canadian honkers within range of a blind was to him.

Thinking about the bighorns made him remember that

184

he had seen more of the sheep directly across the river from Willow Beach than anywhere else.

An idea struck him. "Let's go for a climb this afternoon, Champ. I've been sitting on a boat seat so much the last couple of months that my Levi's are . . ." He stopped to laugh, remembering how his plain-spoken partner, Tom, would have said it, before adding, "butt-sprung."

Webb stopped at the Beach a moment, to change from the rubber sneakers he wore in the boat to heavier leather shoes, before driving across the river and tying up his boat.

At the base of the promontory, he drew upon his hunting skills and walked the bank, going upriver, looking for signs of the sheep: tracks, trails and droppings. All the signs he found were several days old. Then it occurred to

185

him that he hadn't seen any sheep there during the last few days. Thinking about where the bighorns might be, he remembered that Brant had said they could go without water for several days. Perhaps they were up high in the crags.

He followed the bank around the base of the promontory until he came to a little canyon that led away from the river. He walked up this until he could see a ridge that appeared to lead upward. As he followed the ridge that turned left and up into the trio of peaks, the way began to open, and various avenues of gaining the top became apparent.

It was barren, hard rock. At times he had to scramble for a foothold. All the while he had to be alert to keep from running into cactus, but other than this desert growth, there was little vegetation. He wondered just what the bighorns found to eat.

After a little climbing, Webb began to understand why a bighorn trophy was so highly prized. It would be darned hard to get one! It took a lot of man, he realized, when he stopped his climbing for the third time, to rest and catch his breath.

Finally he topped out on the ridge forming the saddle between two of the peaks. There he stopped to look around. The third peak rose in front of him, and to the south. A canyon kept the three peaks from forming a natural crater. He turned to the peak on his left, the one just opposite his camp and the highest of the three. It was the one the osprey used as a roost.

"Let's climb it, Champ," he said to the dog, sending him ahead. He was anxious to see what the river looked like from up there.

As he climbed the rock-studded ridge, he saw numerous

sheep beds. Each of these was fringed with droppings, and he stopped to pick up a few now and then, to crush the pellets between his fingers. They were all dry, several days to a week old. He wondered why there were no fresh ones. The sheep had been there in some numbers, he judged, from the sign they had left.

It took him fifteen minutes to get to the promontory. As he neared it, he saw it was a different formation than it had appeared to be, from the bank on the other side of the river. There was a little cup or pocket right up on top, and he headed for it.

Soon he stood on the edge and looked down on his camp, far below on Willow Beach. He was surprised to see the pattern of his daily activities traced on the sand. There was a well-defined path from his tent to where he beached the boat every day. Another path led through the scattered willows to the skinning cradles, and from there to the curing racks under the ramada.

He studied the other side of the river as a thought struck him. He could find no trace of his route out of the camp toward the ledge and the prospector's tunnel, where he had cached the cured pelts. The route was over hard, barren rock. The tunnel was in fairly plain sight, except for a partial screening of a shoulder of the ledge, and Webb was surprised to see a half-dozen more prospect holes the gold seeker had drilled into the mountain at various places around the outcropping that formed the ledge.

He shook his head when he thought of the amount of work the unknown prospector had done in his unrewarded effort to explore the outcropping and the possibility of finding worthwhile ore.

Webb smiled to see that Champ was busily sniffing at the rock forming the bottom of the pocket. Then the boy leaned out over the escarpment to look at the perch of the osprey below. It was right under him, and he could see it had been abandoned very recently. A partly-eaten trout had dried in the sun.

He was about to turn and continue his hunt for the big-horns, when his sharp eyes spied peculiarly familiar stains on the side of the cliff below. He stared unbelievingly, but they still looked like dried tobacco juice that somebody might have been spitting over the edge!

Webb felt his stomach tightening. He was afraid of what he had to look for, knowing he would surely find it.

Standing still, he searched the bare and broken rock around him. Nothing. He shifted his position a few feet to the right and scanned the pocket again. Then he saw a partially-burned and crushed cigarette stub, down between two rocks. Very carefully he lifted it out. The tip was oval-shaped—Milt's!

Webb felt a chill ripple up his back, into his scalp. He knew the pair had been here, watching the camp below. But how had they managed to get up here without coming by his camp?

The boy looked away from the river toward the two peaks that formed the other points of the triangle. The canyon separating the peaks began at his feet. It went between them and apparently turned to the left. Webb remembered seeing a break in this canyon a ways down-river. That would be the men's approach to this place—their lookout point!

He commanded Champ to follow, and hurried down the mountain the way he had come, then ran along the shore to his boat. It was great fun for Champ, who romped along-side his master. But to Webb it was serious business.

He was certain Milt and Bango had been on the promontory above his camp, at least once. He knew the mouth of the canyon would give him the answers to the questions in his mind.

He made the run downriver in a matter of minutes. The canyon that began inside the three peaks across the river from Willow Beach emptied into the Colorado just above Roaring Rapids.

There he found the story of what had been happening. His eyes, which were trained to follow the faint spoor of a bobcat running up a sand wash, had no trouble interpreting the sign left by the men who had followed the canyon to the promontory. To make sure, he followed their trail a short way.

Bango had gone up the canyon about six different times. The other man had accompanied him once. Webb felt no doubt—the pair had been watching his camp and were planning to steal the beaver pelts!

18

THE FIGHT IN ROARING RAPIDS

That same evening, as soon as it was dark, Webb climbed up to the mining tunnel to satisfy himself that his cache of cured beaver pelts was still there. He was surprised, when he counted them, that there were over one hundred and fifty skins, and that more than ninety of them were silvers.

"Wow!" he exclaimed to himself when he had estimated their worth. "Over seven thousand dollars!"

With this realization came a new wave of concern.

Webb decided then and there to get the pelts ready for Brant. Surely the ranger would soon come. It had now been over a week since the officer had stopped on his way north to investigate the bighorn sheep poaching.

Webb first stacked the pelts into three piles of fifty each, and then he wrapped each of these in waterproofed canvas that Brant had left for that purpose. He lashed each bale tightly with a quarter-inch rope.

It was late when he finished, and he walked to the mouth of the mining tunnel and stood there a while, thinking and listening to the night, watching the stars come out.

He thought back over the days since Brant had stopped, trying to recall exactly what he had done, every day. He was relieved to remember that he had always had his rifle with him. Bango had surely seen this, and that was why they hadn't jumped him.

The men must have decided that the furs were being cached somewhere. Webb wondered if they would know about the mining tunnel, and decided not. He had made all his trips, carrying the cured pelts, at night, well after dark. If they had guessed that he might be hiding the catch in a prospector's hole or under a ledge, they would have to search the more than half-dozen he had seen from the promontory.

As Webb thought, he stood well back in the tunnel, looking out the mouth of it, and he was surprised at how well he could see the beach and his route back to camp, even though it was dark.

The white sand of the beach and the river reflected the light of the stars, and even of the moon, which was still out of sight behind the surrounding mountains. The whole scene had a ghostly appearance and the scattered clumps of willows seemed to float in it. An involuntary shudder swept up Webb's tall frame.

"Little scary, huh, Champ?" he whispered, stepping around the dog, who sat in front of him, and out of the tunnel.

A thought played persistently in his mind while he walked back to camp, and when he got there he rolled up his bed and threw it across his shoulders. Taking his rifle, he went back up to the ledge and rolled out his bed in the mouth of the mining tunnel.

He felt safe there, with Champ curled up at his feet. The alert dog would warn him of anything unusual. Still,

191

his imagination would not rest, and it was well toward morning when he finally decided what he would do.

He would get out before daylight, and as soon as there was light enough to see, he would run Crane's Nest Rapids and the Ring Bolt, then look at his traps and spring them all, take whatever beaver he had caught and bring them to camp. Then he would stay on guard until Brant came back. He would finish trapping the river after the ranger had picked up the cured furs.

In spite of the fact that he had made up his mind and laid his plans, he still couldn't sleep. Time after time he got up to look at the sky. Finally the Great Dipper disappeared below the horizon, and the moon passed over and out of sight behind the promontory across the river, so Webb knew it was almost morning.

He hurried down and through the camp, got into his boat and pushed off. A cold, clammy wind blew hard down the canyon, and he shivered in the early morning gloom as he faced it. He had to hold the motor at half-speed in his run up the river, because of the darkness in the canyon.

At Crane's Nest he waited impatiently for enough light to run the rough water, and even though he was successful, he knew he had left his camp too soon and was risking his life in this dangerous spot.

Anxiety rose in him as he ran up into the tail of the race at Ring Bolt. He had a feeling now that he should have stayed on guard in the camp. He had half made up his mind to turn back, when he began wondering how many beaver he would have in the traps above the rapids. Probably a good catch. And if there were many silvers, it would be a waste if he didn't get them skinned and stretched, for the hides would spoil if left too long, and the precious fur would slip.

Without thinking further, he gave the motor full throttle for a try at the Ring Bolt.

He knew he had made a mistake the moment he swung the boat over to climb up on the crest of the Ring Bolt. He miscalculated in the dim light and turned into the full sweep of the river too soon! The torrent caught the prow of the boat and swept it sidewise into the rough water below the lip. The lightly-laden craft pitched hard, and Webb knew he'd have to ride it out. Water cascaded over the stern, drowning out the motor and drenching Webb and Champ.

As soon as he floated out on the smoother water below, Webb rowed away from the main channel and nosed the boat into the bank. It took him a full forty minutes to dry out the ignition system to where he could start the motor again. It burst into an uneven roar, and Webb sighed relief as it settled down.

The twenty traps above the Ring Bolt held twelve beaver, all silvers, and Webb felt glad he had decided to come up. He sprung the other eight traps and turned the boat downstream, opening the throttle.

Champ rode on the deck, the wind whipping his ears and an expression of pleasure on his face.

The moment Webb drove the boat onto the beach he knew his camp had been visited. The sand was wet where someone had splashed ashore!

His first thought was of the cache. Forgetting secrecy, he ran up to the ledge and plunged into the tunnel. The bales of pelts were gone!

Even as he ran back, Champ at his side, he could read the tracks and tell what had happened. Two men had been there, one of them Bango, because he saw where the tank boss had spat several times. It was not hard to spot where the bales of furs had been loaded into the boat, either.

And Webb stumbled with a surge of fear as he read in the sand the mute story of his close and unrealized escape. Bango had sneaked up on the camp, coming from down the river. Webb could see where the tank boss had dropped in the sand behind a group of willows as he—Webb—had trotted through camp to his boat . . . where the tank boss had started to run after him, then changed his mind as he had figured out where and why Webb had spent the night away from camp.

Webb knew why neither he nor Champ had heard or seen Bango. It was because of the strong wind blowing down the canyon, and because of the soft, quiet sand on the beach!

Unwittingly, he had fooled the tank boss by leaving before daylight.

The full realization of what had almost happened to him that morning filled Webb with a new resolve. Suddenly he felt himself a man, equal to this man's challenge. He ran to his boat and threw the beaver carcasses out onto the beach. He worked with a quiet, but desperate hurry, to lighten the boat.

Webb knew the hijackers had to be downstream. They had come by boat and had left the same way.

As he checked his rifle and loaded his shotgun, he tried to think of what Bango might do. Their purpose had been to rob the camp of the furs. And now they had to get them out—off the river.

There was only one place close to Willow Beach where a road contacted the river. That was at the mouth of El Dorado Canyon, twelve miles below Willow Beach and six miles below Roaring Rapids.

Webb knew he had to beat them there!

194

He commanded Champ into the bottom and pushed the boat off into the current. The motor burst into a full-throated roar. Then Webb was thankful he had been forced to check the ignition and clean the sparkplugs that morning. Maybe now he would get the breaks he needed!

He rode the channel of the river, taking advantage of every current as he searched ahead for signs of the other boat. When he came in sight of the beginning of Roaring Rapids, his heart sank. The other craft was nowhere in sight.

But, even as he looked, he saw Bango guide his boat out of a sheltering cove that had been screened by willows. Milt was still bending over the bales of pelts, just finishing shifting them, to balance the craft before they entered Roaring Rapids.

Webb knew neither Bango nor Milt had heard him, because of the noise of their own motor and the rising thunder of Roaring Rapids.

The boy's boat gained rapidly on the more heavily-laden craft. Webb thought of his rifle, and raised it. But the reality of shooting a human being was suddenly impossible. There must be another—a better way!

Bango and Milt were both watching their approach into Roaring Rapids. Webb rifled his own craft in behind them. He was within a dozen yards when Bango turned around.

The poachers' boat paused in a backlash. Webb instinctively pulled the tiller over, to keep from crashing into the motor on the stern of the other boat, and slid alongside. Milt looked around in astonishment at the sudden appearance of Webb's boat.

The boy throttled back, fighting to stay behind. But his lighter craft was caught on the crest and swept ahead. He

The boy made his decision. He jammed the

throttle over and turned his boat into the current

could only risk a sidewise glance as the two boats dropped onto the rolling, tumbling water, side by side.

Then he knew he was in a tight place. The pillar of rock which split Roaring Rapids loomed ahead.

Bango saw it too. And Webb heard the tank boss give his motor full throttle. The gunnels crashed together as Bango turned into Webb's boat, forcing him over.

Webb saw the man's plan: to crash him into the pillar of rock! Then he remembered the passage in the reef! He gassed his motor and his boat leaped ahead, sliding away from the other craft. Milt reached out to hold it, while Bango fought to turn Webb into the onrushing rock.

The boy smashed his closed fist down on Milt's hand and momentarily the other lost his grip. It was enough! Webb slipped by the massive pillar.

He shot through the passageway with an inch to spare on either side. Bango's boat jerked back out of his vision, and Webb heard it crash on the rock fingers combing the swiftly-flowing water which surged around the pillar.

As the boy turned into the eddy behind the huge rock, he saw the other boat rolling and filling. The water poured in as it capsized. The white, foaming water smothered the tank boss's scream as the tiller of the heavy motor caught him and dragged him under.

Webb saw the bales of pelts spill out and float by. And then he saw Milt bob up, his arms flailing awkwardly. A glance in his own boat showed Webb that Champ was low in the craft and riding out the excitement like a veteran.

The boy made his decision. He jammed the throttle over and turned his boat into the current. He ran up on the drowning man and spun the motor halfway around. The reverse thrust stopped the craft inches from Milt's head, and the instant it did, Webb shut off the motor. He scrambled across the boat seat and onto the deck, tossing the tie rope to the sinking man. Milt's searching, clawing hands found it.

Webb scrambled back in the boat and started the motor, and with Milt dragging on the tie rope, he swung back into the eddy and came up behind the pillar of rock, a plan forming in his mind as he completed the rescue.

This was a different Webb Dodge from the boy that anyone had ever seen before. He hardly knew himself as he forced Milt to let go of the rope and climb up on the jagged pillar of rock dividing Roaring Rapids.

He swung his boat away from the marooned contrabander and out into the current again. A half mile downstream, he spied Bango's craft, floating bottom up. Even before he got near enough to turn the wooden hull over, he saw what had happened. The rock fingers of the reef had torn a long gash in the hull, caught the motor, tearing it and the transom off the boat.

Webb guided his boat back and forth across the river, drifting downstream with Bango's craft, while he searched for the man. As he looked and looked, he felt mixed emotions for the tank boss who had tried three different times to kill him.

Long after he knew there was no hope of finding Bango alive, Webb was still searching, and it was then that he discovered the bales of pelts floating down the river. The air which was caught in the fur and between the pelts and in the canvas tarps he had tied so securely had kept them afloat.

It took him thirty minutes to work them all in to the bank of the river and to get them into his boat.

Then he started back upstream, traveling slowly, swinging back and forth, still looking for Bango. But there was no sign of the tank boss.

Finally he reached the tail of Roaring Rapids again, and he looked ahead to the pillar of rock.

Milt was still clinging to it, half his body out of water.

19

THE REWARD

Webb nosed his boat up to the terrified Milt.

"Crawl back on the deck," he commanded, "and lie down. Don't try to get back into the boat!" He raised the shotgun significantly.

He was surprised at the change in Milt, the confident, sophisticated man who had tried to bribe him into smuggling beaver pelts. All the cocksureness the dark little man had shown in the motel was gone. The fixer for the contraband fur dealers cringed on the deck, dripping water. His hands were white with strain as he clung to the gunnels while Webb turned his boat into the fast water and headed up through Roaring Rapids.

Once through the rough water, Webb called Champ to the stern.

"All right now, get into the boat," he said to the terrified man. "Turn around and sit down. One phony move and I'll send this dog at you!"

Champ had changed as much as Webb had. The big dog was no longer the well-mannered, quiet retriever. It was plain that he remembered the beating Savote had given him, and he associated Milt with that incident. He stood now, head lowered, hackles raised, growling deep in his throat.

Milt inched off the deck and onto the front seat.

"Down, Champ," Webb said. The dog became quiet, but did not relax his vigilance.

Milt spoke over his shoulder, slowly, hesitatingly at first, and then pleading as he went on. "Listen, Webb, we gave you a bad time. Sure. But it was Savote. Now you've got me cold. What's your price? Just name it. Any kind of a deal."

"No deal with me . . . of any kind . . . at any price."

The way Webb said it conveyed the state of his mind. The tone was flat, unemotional. There was no compromise to be made. Milt recognized this and sat silent as they sped up the river toward Willow Beach.

Webb's spirits lifted when he came in sight of his camp. He had been wondering what he was going to do with Milt, how to hold him. But there was no need to worry about that now.

He could see Brant's car. The game ranger had come!

As Webb came closer, he saw still another car pulled up on the other side of Brant's, and then even a third, half-hidden behind his tent.

A half-dozen men were there. The relief the boy felt made him realize how far he was from being the completely tough, self-reliant man he had felt himself to be a few minutes earlier. He saw Brant walk away from the group and come down to the shore. Judge Schaulkler was close behind, and then Webb recognized the familiar head-tilted stance of Tom Jesson!

The three strangers stayed near the fire they had built

on the beach, until Brant called to them. He turned back to Webb.

"Hi, Kid!" greeted the ranger, his face showing puzzlement at the presence of the bedraggled Milt in the front of Webb's boat. "What's going on?"

Webb grinned self-consciously and ran the boat onto the sand, ordering Milt out. Champ was behind him, and took his stance watchfully at his master's side.

"Here's the fellow who tried to arrange that deal with me that night in Needles. His name is Milt Krakow." Webb's voice was firm as he faced Brant.

The ranger's mouth dropped open, then it closed before splitting into a wide, gold-set smile.

"Well, what d'ya know! Mr. Krakow, I want you to meet Mr. Ralph Hall, a law-enforcement agent for the U. S. Fish and Wildlife Service. You two will probably have a lot to talk about when you get better acquainted."

A tall, uniformed man stepped out from the group of men Webb didn't know.

Then Brant grabbed Webb by the hand. "Hey, am I glad to see you!" he exclaimed. "You had me worried—plenty! I caught those sheep poachers I was after and had to take them in to Kingman to file charges, so I couldn't get back here. Then everybody showed up and wanted to see the windup of the beaver trapping on the river. But when we got here you were gone, and so was the catch. We had it partly figured out, but weren't sure what had happened to you—not until you showed up from downriver." Not quite winded by this long speech, Brant turned to the other two strangers, saying, "Frank, here's your beaver trapper. Webb, this is Mr. Frank Parker, the Director of the Arizona Game and Fish Commission . . . and here's Mr. Lee Thorpe, chairman of the Commissioners. . . . Mr. Thorpe, Webb Dodge, the best beaver skinner in the West. . . ." Brant looked sidewise at Tom, and added, "That is, next to Tom Jesson!" Then he gave a delighted laugh.

The two gray-haired men, one thin, the other heavy-set and broad, shook hands with Webb, and the boy felt embarrassed as they looked at him closely. He knew they were sizing him up.

Brant reached up to put an arm across his shoulders, asserting, "Webb will measure up to everything I told you about him. He'll make a hand in anybody's outfit, and I hope it will be in mine."

Webb couldn't remember everything that happened after that, one thing followed another in such quick succession. Tom helped him unload the bales of pelts and open them and hang the skins up to dry, while Brant cooked supper.

It was then that Tom told Webb about the new Division of Fur Conservation that had been set up within the state's game department, and about Brant's being made the chief of the division.

Webb felt elated at the news of the good things which were happening for Brant.

"Means lots of work for me," grumped Tom. "Brant's got a lot of newfangled ideas about live-trappin' the beaver and turnin' 'em loose on streams that ain't got any." Here he tilted his head sharply to bring Webb within vision of his good eye. "Might make sense, at that, though." The pair worked silently for a few moments, and Webb's thoughts were whirling.

Tom spoke again. "Ain't the only changes. . . . There's plenty comin' up for you. If you wuz aimin', like I told you to, you sure hit what you aimed at!"

The old man refused to elaborate on this tantalizing statement, and it wasn't until they were all gathered around the campfire that evening, discussing the eventful day, that things began to fall into place and make sense for Webb.

Director Frank Parker said, "Ralph will take Milt Krakow in to Kingman, to file formal charges. Ralph tells me Milt has agreed to turn government's witness. That will mean the breakup of that whole organization, from the beaver poachers here in the West, clear through to the group of fur garment-makers in New York who have been conspiring with them." The man looked across the fire to Webb, declaring, "It's quite a thing you did, Webb, breaking up a nation-wide ring of illegal fur dealers and coat-makers. Rich Savote had a real setup! You're to be congratulated, even if you can't get a reward for your good work."

Judge Schaulkler, sitting next to Webb, placed a hand gently on the boy's knee, but he spoke across the fire to the director.

"I'm certain that reward will come to Webb in some form or another. It always does come to the man who does a job well, as Webb has done during these past few months!"

The boy squirmed, uneasy at being the center of attention. He was glad it was getting dark because the skin of his face felt hot and must be red.

The jurist reached into his inside pocket and took out some legal papers. "I was cleaning my files today and disposing of some old cases when Brant came by to bring me up here," he said overcasually. "I haven't had a chance to destroy this one; think I'll do it now." He held the papers a moment, seeming to consider what to do with them. Then he handed them to Webb. "Would you mind putting these on the fire for me, Webb?" He smiled gravely. "You're younger than I am. Thanks!"

Webb rolled up on one knee to place the sheaf of papers on the campfire. The light caught the printing and he read:

"WEBB DODGE,
ward of the Juvenile Division
of the
Mohave County Superior Court."

He looked around quickly at the judge, who smiled up at him with a warmth that wasn't the campfire reflected in his eyes. The jurist continued filling and tamping the tobacco into his pipe as he spoke in a sonorous and judicial manner.

"Please carry out the order of the Court!"

The heat of the flames curled the papers before they caught fire, and then suddenly they were gone. Webb was watching so intently through his filling eyes that he didn't notice the men get to their feet until the judge spoke again.

"There is another matter, Webb—about your dog. I was successful in tracing that registration marker, and I found his former owner all right. However, it isn't in my jurisdiction to take it up with you, I am sure of that. So I think I'll retire now and let your best friend tell you about it." The judge turned to the others. "Gentlemen, I propose that we . . . hit the sack!"

After the others had left, the compact little ranger, balancing on his toes on the far side of the campfire, was left with Webb. Brant smiled as he stepped around the flaming driftwood.

"That was a full pardon, Webb. You just burned your record. . . . You knew that, didn't you?"

Webb couldn't speak. All the pent-up emotions within him seemed to be coming out of his eyes. He could hardly understand what the ranger was saying. There was one thought uppermost in his mind.

"What about Champ, Brant? What about him? I thought you promised . . ."

The ranger took a folded paper from between the leaves of a notebook. His expression was hidden from the boy. He spoke soberly. "Before I go into that, I want to tell you what else the judge has done for you. . . ."

Webb's eyes were on the paper as Brant went on. "I told you the judge was a sportsman . . . one of the rare ones, Webb. He's a vice-president and a member of the board of directors of the Arizona Game Protective Association—that's a state-wide organization of hunters and fishermen." Webb moved restlessly, but listened as Brant went on. "He proposed that this group set up a conservation scholarship fund—money to send a boy through school, even college." Brant balled his fist and jabbed Webb in the shoulder muscles. "And guess what, Kid? You're it! He recommended you for the first award. That makes it a cinch as far as you're concerned, of course. You've got it made!"

"Please, Brant!" pleaded Webb. "What about Champ? Do I have to give him up?"

The ranger shook his head. "No! I checked and that fellow won't ask to have him back." He put the paper in Webb's eager hand.

The boy had to stoop down to get the light of the dying fire on the paper as he unfolded it, to read:

"Golden Boy, general description, yellow Labrador Retriever, yellow eyes, registration marks, five tattooed dots in left ear,
Pedigree. . . . .
Owner: Brant Murphy."

Through tear-filled eyes, Webb managed to read an addition to the script, "Title to the Golden Boy is hereby transferred to: Webb Dodge." He looked up and across the glowing coals of the campfire as the game ranger turned away and walked toward his tent.

A cold nose pushed in under Webb's arm, and a warm, rough-coated body wriggled in close as a gust of wind came off the river and stirred a tiny, bright flame out of the glowing coals of the nearly-dead fire.

CHARLEY NIEHUIS

was born on the banks of Beaver Creek in Buck Grove, Iowa. While his brothers and sisters followed more traditional ways of making a living, the author share-operated a popcorn machine in Austin, Minnesota, worked as copy boy on the old *Arizona Gazette* in Phoenix, Arizona, bellhopped and barbered his way from Cedar Rapids, Iowa, to Prescott, Arizona. There he began photographing the out-of-doors and writing about hunting and fishing, his favorite sports, while he served as "stringer" for United Press.

His first outdoor story appeared in *Sports Afield,* in 1939. Since then he has continued his hunting and fishing in the Southwest and writing about his experiences for *Sports Illustrated, True's Fishing* and *Hunting Yearbooks, Outdoor Life, Sports Afield, Field and Stream, Better Homes and Gardens, Bluebook* and other magazines.

Charley Niehuis is also credited with the setting up of the Division of Information and Education for the Arizona Game and Fish Commission. He headed this organization until he resigned, to serve as executive secretary for the state's organized sportsmen, the Arizona Game Protective Association, and to edit its magazine, the *Arizona Wildlife-Sportsman.*

The author has an intense interest in conservation of natural resources—including the boyhood of the young men of our nation. His own three boys, Barry, David and Paul, and their friends, have often shared his outdoor adventures while hunting and fishing. His first book for teen-agers, *Trapping the Silver Beaver,* combines these enthusiasms, with a special bow to his birthplace!